Battle for Cascadia

September 2011

Battle for Cascadia

The Second Book of The Gaia Wars

Kenneth G. Bennett

One

"Where are we exactly?" Mirra asked, her voice soft and fragile.

It was sunrise, and she was standing on a wild ridge, gazing down into a broad ocean of fog. Slender waterfalls on nearby mountainsides glistened through fissures in the mist.

The morning was cool, the sky overhead clear. It was going to be a fine June day.

"We're deep inside North Cascades National Park," said Ina. "About thirteen miles from the nearest road."

Mirra studied Ina closely, then turned slowly, three hundred and sixty degrees, taking in the whole landscape. She looked at the spot where she'd woken up minutes earlier. Warren Wilkes and a boy she didn't recognize were asleep on the grass. The boys looked peaceful in their sleeping bags.

"But I don't understand," she said, rubbing her temples as she spoke. "Thirteen miles from the nearest road? How can that be?"

"We walked here. Thaddeus carried you."

"Who?" Mirra laughed. "Carried me? What are you talking about?"

Ina led Mirra to a different vantage point, slightly higher up. From here they could look down the opposite side of the ridge. Pristine alpine meadow graced the upper five hundred feet of this slope. Below that stood dense thickets of alder and scrub. Steep chutes choked with boulders and loose scree broke the carpet of green. Farther down, lush emerald forest blanketed a broad, U-shaped valley. There was hardly any fog on this side of the ridge.

Mirra saw movement a hundred feet below where they were standing: two men working intently amid a thicket of low, barrel shapes.

Mirra couldn't figure out the "barrels." They didn't look man-made, really, but they didn't appear natural, either. She squinted. Some of the barrels were bubbling; steaming at the top.

"The big man is Thaddeus," said Ina. "The tall, lean one is Achak. My brother."

"Your brother?" said Mirra absently, as if this fact combined with everything else she was seeing added up to too many things to process. "Ina," she said thickly, "can you please tell me what's going on? I have the most horrific headache."

"I'm not surprised," said Ina, "the amount of drugs you had in your system."

Mirra turned on her sharply. "Drugs?"

Ina stepped to a rock covered with camping gear and

picked up a bowl of granola. Tugging open her pack, she removed a small box of milk, punctured the top of the little container with the attached straw, and squirted the milk into the cereal.

"I added thimbleberries," she said, handing Mirra the bowl and a spoon. "From the meadow. Please eat. It will make you feel better. There's coffee, too."

Mirra took the cereal and tore into it. She was famished.

Ina said, "Mirra, what's the last thing you remember … from yesterday?"

Mirra turned and stared down into the fog-shrouded valley. "I was sitting in the sunroom … a little before five, I think. Alvin Peeples brought me a chamomile tea, the dear man."

"The tea," said Ina, "was the first dose. They injected you with something else in the truck."

"What?" Mirra laughed, and put down her spoon. "What are you talking about? Why would someone drug me?"

The sun peeked above a distant ridge, bathing the meadows in golden light. Thaddeus and Achak paused from their toil amid the "barrels." Warm rays glinted off the tops of some of them.

Mirra squinted again. She could swear the structures were growing. Expanding. Almost as she watched. They definitely seemed bigger than the first time she'd looked.

"Peeples drugged you so that he could kidnap you," said Ina matter-of-factly. "He had help from two other men. As they were fleeing Ridgecrest, they also kidnapped Warren and Sean Gibson." Ina pointed. "Sean is the other boy sleeping over there."

Mirra laughed again. The story sounded absurd. But Ina's expression never changed.

"But old Mr. Peeples?" sputtered Mirra. "That's crazy! He's nice to me. He's my friend. Why would he do such a thing? How could he do such a thing? Alvin Peeples is old. Frail. It's preposterous!"

"He didn't just drug and kidnap you," Ina said. "He also set fire to Ridgecrest, to cover his tracks and create a distraction."

The incredulous smile vanished from Mirra's face. "What? No! It's not true. None of this is true. You and Alvin don't get along. This is about that, isn't it? About …"

"It's all true," said Ina. "I swear to you."

"But it makes no sense," said Mirra, tears welling in her eyes and panic rising in her voice. "Everything's okay at Ridgecrest, right? They caught the fire in time."

Ina took Mirra's hand. "Most of Ridgecrest was destroyed," she said. "I followed Peeples as he fled with you, so I don't have all the answers. But the fire was bad."

"But all my friends," Mirra cried. "Ms. Grivner."

"Warren saw Ms. Grivner standing on the street," said Ina. "He said she was fine. He said there were lots of residents around her."

The story rendered Mirra speechless for several seconds. "Peeples was sick, then," she said at last, almost to herself. "Mentally ill. There's no other explanation." She stopped. "But you said he had help."

"Peeples was following orders," said Ina.

Mirra stared at her. "Orders?"

"For many years, Peeples's job was simply to keep an eye on you. Track your movements. Observe. Then he got new orders. He learned that his master was coming back."

"His what?" said Mirra, disgusted now. "Ina, what the hell is going on? Look, if Peeples and these others really kidnapped us, they obviously failed, right? We're with you, and ..." she gestured at the men working amid the barrels, "whatever their names are."

"Thaddeus and Achak."

"Thaddeus and Achak. But why did you bring us here? To the middle of nowhere? We should be in town. Helping our friends."

"We had to come here," said Ina. "For your sake."

"My sake?" said Mirra, studying her friend, trying to read her expression. "What? Because of the kidnappers? Don't tell me we're running from Alvin Peeples. Where are the police?"

"I don't think the police can help us," said a soft voice behind them. It was Warren.

Two

Ina and Mirra turned to find Warren Wilkes tugging a fleece jacket on over a very wrinkled shirt. He looked lean and strong, and wild, with his long, uncombed hair and sparkling eyes.

"Warren!" Mirra cried. She gave the boy a warm hug. "You're part of all this? You were kidnapped?"

"Yeah," he said, holding her gaze. Studying her face. His mother's face. He smiled as he looked at her.

"Ina's trying to explain ..." Mirra stammered. "But I ... Why are you smiling like that?"

"I can't help it," said Warren, smiling even more. "It's just, you know, all these years ... since I was a toddler, I thought you were ..."

"Warren!" said Ina. "One thing at a time, please. She doesn't know about that yet."

"Doesn't know about what yet?" said Mirra. "What sort of conspiracy is this?"

"You were asking about the police," said Ina, changing the subject. "Warren told you they can't help us. And he's right."

Mirra looked from Ina to Warren and back. "Why not? The police can't handle a deranged old man?"

"Alvin Peeples is a soldier," said Ina. "One soldier, in an army. An army bent on recapturing you."

"So now there's an army after us." Mirra sighed and studied her companions again. "This is some enormous game, isn't it? I just haven't figured it out yet."

"It's not a game," Warren said softly. "There is an army coming. And they all have the same abilities as these guys." He gestured at Ina, and at the two men working down slope.

Mirra stared at him. "Oh? And what abilities are those?"

Ina sighed, stepped to a garbage-can-sized boulder half buried in the dirt, ripped it out of the ground, and lifted it effortlessly over her head.

Mirra gasped and dropped her cereal bowl.

Ina leaned her head back, opened her mouth, and emitted three firecracker-loud clicks.

The clicks made Thaddeus and Achak jerk to attention amid the barrels. Ina squatted, then exploded upward, launching the boulder seventy-five feet into the air.

Thaddeus stepped away from the barrels and watched the boulder intently, tracking it like an outfielder tracking a fly ball.

Mirra cried out. The meteor-like chunk was heading straight for him. He'd be killed! He'd be ...

Thaddeus caught the boulder. Caught it. Adjusted it in his hands. Steadied it. Then he squatted, exploded upward, and fired the huge rock like some mythical three-point shot. The great stone travelled a tremendous arc, hundreds of feet, before finally it crashed like a wrecking ball amid the alders, booming and thundering until it came to rest at last.

Mirra's face was pale.

"This isn't real," she said quietly. She sat on a rock and pulled her jacket tight around her. "None of this is real."

Warren sat down next to her and gently took her hand. "It is real," he said. "I couldn't believe it either at first. But I've seen things the last few days ... learned things ..."

Thaddeus signaled to Ina.

"He wants us to start moving our stuff under the trees soon," she said.

Warren squeezed his mother's hand and looked her in the eye. "Mirra," he said firmly. "You have to trust what you're seeing. And trust what Ina is saying. You have to."

Mirra stared at him. Shook her head. "But ... so ... why would Peeples and these others kidnap me? Us? And why would they follow us here? I don't have any money. I don't have ..."

"They want you," Ina said, "because of who you are."

"What does that mean?" Mirra asked, exasperated.

Ina started to answer, then turned and stared down into the fog-shrouded valley. Collected her thoughts.

"Mirra," she said at last. "Why have you been living at Ridgecrest?"

"Because I like it there." The question seemed to irritate Mirra.

"But you're a young woman. You're smart. You're beautiful. Why don't you have a career or a family?" Why don't you have a life? Why live at Ridgecrest with all those old people?"

Mirra's reply was concise. "I need to heal."

"Heal from what?"

Mirra fidgeted and turned away, voice rising. "I don't want to talk about that. This isn't about my problems. You're turning things around. This isn't about me."

"It is completely, one hundred percent about you," Ina replied, emphasizing each word. Mirra was seated on the rock and Ina dropped to her knees before her.

"You survived a horrific attack, Mirra. So horrific that you forced yourself to forget what happened. I understand. We all do.

"He tried to break you. He nearly succeeded. But I know the real you is still there. The memory lives, deep inside you. And we need you to face it now. You must face it. It is our only hope."

"No," said Mirra.

And Warren could have sworn that her voice was suddenly coming from every direction. From the ground. From the surrounding ridges and forest. From the meadows. It boomed and bounced like a supersonic echo.

The ridge shook, so abruptly and violently that Warren was thrown to the ground. Huge slabs of rock broke from jagged cliffs on the opposite ridge, separating and falling, in what seemed like slow motion. Thaddeus and Achak dropped to hands and knees amid the cocoons, scrambling to stabilize the sloshing cylinders.

"Earthquake!" Sean cried, his sleeping bag falling to his knees as he leapt up. His thick hair looked like it had been styled with a blender, and he was still half asleep. He fell sideways and clutched a bush as the ridge continued to heave and buck.

Huge plumes of dust rose, as rocks shifted and the Earth settled.

Mirra looked more startled than anyone. "An earthquake," she said, almost to herself. Ina was watching her, smiling.

"Something funny?" said Mirra angrily. "Why are you looking at me like that? That was a big quake."

"I know."

Mirra stared at her. "But we should report it or something. That was bad. That was …"

"That was you," said Ina, smiling once more.

Mirra laughed. "Me?"

Achak clicked suddenly, high and sharp. CLICK! CLICK! CLICK!

"Let's move!" said Ina. "Under the trees. People coming."

Thaddeus and Achak sprinted into camp, scattering the little fire ring and scooping up gear as Ina and Warren helped.

Sean pulled on a pair of pants, gawking at his companions and his surroundings.

Thaddeus fell to his knees before Mirra, a pile of haphazardly-gathered gear in his arms.

"Goddess," he rumbled, bowing his head. "It is a great joy to see you well. To see you reclaiming your power."

Achak bowed also. "Goddess," he said.

"We haven't gotten that far yet, guys," Ina called, as she shoved Sean toward the trees. "She doesn't know what you're talking about."

Thaddeus and Achak bowed again, awkwardly, then continued collecting gear.

Warren took Mirra's hand. "I think they want us under

the trees," he said. "Like, right now." He heard the drone of an airplane and saw Thaddeus glance skyward.

Ina scooped up the remaining items from the sleeping area and sprinted for the trees, just as the plane cleared the far ridge. There was no evidence the camp had existed.

Down slope, Thaddeus and Achak had positioned rocks and brush to conceal the hatchery, without blocking any daylight. The glistening cylinders were already bathed in full sun, but the area around the bizarre growths looked natural, undisturbed. The airplane buzzed louder.

"The airplane," said Warren. "That's what you were warning about?"

Achak had climbed a few feet up a scrubby cedar tree and was gazing north, toward the Clearwater lookout. "No," he replied. "Though we don't want to be seen by a plane, either. But I was talking about people on foot."

Warren studied the long, undulating ridge leading to the fire tower. The ridge looked empty. Nothing but open alpine meadow for miles. But Warren knew from experience that there were notches and folds in the ridge where animals and people could hide.

"There's a group coming from the tower," said Achak, gazing out.

"Agents?" said Thaddeus. "Fabrinels?"

Achak shook his head. "No. Children."

"Children?" said Ina.

"Seven or eight kids. Three adults. They're headed straight for us."

Three

Six miles away, FBI agent Owen Moss was studying Uhlgoth and a cluster of Fabrinels through binoculars. He said, "I got out of bed at 3:30 in the morning for *this*? Terrific use of tax dollars."

He unclipped a satellite phone from his belt and turned to the young agent nearby. "It's one of those stupid reenactment things," he said, gesturing down valley.

The junior agent stared through his own binoculars. Long fingers of tattered mist clung to the valley floor and Uhlgoth and his soldiers seemed to vanish and reappear as they traversed the landscape one thousand yards below. The swarm was moving fast, running across open spaces, leaping creeks and fallen trees. They carried weapons: spears, bows and arrows, hatchets.

"Something's wrong with the faces," said the junior agent, whose name was Josh Flynn. "Looks like some of 'em are wearing masks."

Moss finished a swig of coffee from his thermos cup. "They *are* wearing masks," he said. "It's part of the reenactment, I guarantee ya."

"What are they reenacting?" asked Flynn, binoculars still pressed firmly against his eyes.

"Who the hell knows? Some guys dress up like Lewis and Clark. Some pretend to be knights in armor. Freaking bizarre if you ask me." He spit on the ground. "I knew a guy ... missed the entire NFL regular season doing this. Didn't see a *single* game." He paused. Thought about it. "Even if I wanted to do it, I couldn't."

"Why's that?"

"Wife would kill me."

Flynn laughed. "Yeah, so, reenactment ... but the bucket truck ... the fire ... the missing boys ..."

"Yeah?" said Moss, nodding down valley. "These ain't our guys. I'd bet my house they're not kidnappers. And that's sure as heck not a terrorist cell. Unless terrorists have reverted to Stone Age weapons."

He punched a number into the satellite phone and put the device to his ear. "Chief," he said, after a few seconds. "It's Owen. Got a visual on the target but it's the wrong target."

Flynn was still staring through the binoculars. "Heck of a lot of guys down there, Owen," he said softly. "Mostly heading east. But a group just split off. Sorta running ... this way. I lost 'em in the trees." He panned back and forth, trying to find the runners again.

Moss was on the phone and didn't hear him. "Definitely divert the choppers if you can," he was saying. "Use 'em someplace else. Total waste of time in here."

Flynn heard the sudden rumble of army transport helicopters clearing the far ridge. "Too late," he said to Owen. "Cavalry's here."

Something down valley caught his eye. "Hey, check this out."

Moss picked up his own binoculars and followed his gaze. "Chief," he said into the phone, "choppers are here. I'll call you back." He shut the phone and saw what Flynn was looking at.

The swarm had halted mid-valley, and Uhlgoth's soldiers were staring at the choppers floating along the ridge. Flynn raised his binoculars to the choppers and saw armed soldiers in fatigues through open doors. "That looks serious," he said.

Moss shrugged. "Special forces out of Fort Lewis. Tomkin called 'em up. Overkill in my opinion, but he wanted 'em here in case there really was a cell moving down out of Canada. Covering his behind, basically."

The choppers rolled off the ridge and dropped lower into the wide valley.

"They don't much like the helicopters," said Flynn, gesturing downhill.

Some of Uhlgoth's soldiers held their spears aloft, heads back, bellowing defiantly.

Moss chuckled. "Of course not. They're messing up the reenactment. No helicopters in the Middle Ages." Both men laughed.

But as they watched, one of the Fabrinels leaned back and heaved his spear. The weapon accelerated like a missile, crossing the five hundred yard gap between spear thrower and lead chopper in a couple of seconds. Flynn gasped. Through his binoculars he saw the helmeted chopper pilot turn his head. He saw the metal spear tip flash in the morning sun. Then an explosion rocked the valley and a fireball filled the sky where the chopper had been.

Moss and Flynn jumped. "Holy Lord," Moss moaned, reaching absently for his satellite phone. "Holy Lord."

Flynn saw the second chopper bank hard to the left. It dipped. Zoomed forward. Tilting the binoculars down he saw another Fabrinel warrior take aim and throw another spear.

The spear streaked skyward. Impossibly far. Impossibly fast. It slammed into the second chopper's tail rotor and detonated.

"No!" Flynn cried. "No!"

It took a second for the roar of the explosion to reach them and by that time chunks of the flaming craft were raining onto the forest like orange confetti.

Moss was shouting into his phone now. "Mayday! Mayday! Mayday! Two choppers down at marker six-nine-eight-seven-one. I repeat, two choppers down!"

"Owen!" Flynn screamed, tossing his binoculars aside and scooping up his automatic rifle.

Two hundred yards down-slope, Blank Frames were exploding from the trees; barreling uphill, straight for them. The same Fabrinels Flynn had seen splintering from the main swarm minutes earlier.

Flynn raised his weapon. Moss did the same.

What they were seeing was impossible. Olympic sprinters could not have crossed the valley as quickly as these runners had. And yet here they were, flying uphill, knives and hatchets out, yellow eyes flashing.

The agents fired and the runners halted before a blizzard of bullets. Halted; but did not fall.

Instead they bent and twisted and undulated, feet bolted to the ground, as if they were made of rubber or sponge.

Small trees around the Fabrinels shredded and exploded in the firestorm, spitting fountains of wood chips into the air. But the Fabrinels showed no mark. No blood. No pain. Panic seized the agents as their ammunition ran out and the Blank Frames leapt forward, clicking and crackling like fireworks on the Fourth of July.

Four

A thousand yards down slope, Todd Finley Jr. stood, pale and shaking, his plump face now shockingly drawn, his smug smirk replaced by a glazed, perpetually terrified stare, his eyes red from crying and lack of sleep. He'd been thinking about food all night long as he clung to the back of the giant sprinting Fabrinel. But what he'd witnessed just now had destroyed his appetite.

He stumbled sideways, suppressed the urge to vomit, and forced himself to look up again. The tail section of one of the choppers was wedged in tree branches fifty yards away. Bright orange flames danced against the drifting fog. The flames blackened the metal and charred the tree.

The forest was wet. The fire wouldn't spread.

There was a loud crash as another chunk of helicopter burned through branches and smashed to the ground. Todd Jr. jumped.

He'd seen the soldiers in those helicopters. They'd been *that close*. At first, he'd prayed they would land and negotiate with his father; that he and his dad would climb into the craft and fly back to town and that soon he'd be home eating a huge breakfast and watching cartoons.

Then his father had given a simple command.

"Bring them down," he'd said, and to Todd Jr.'s horror, a couple of the Fabrinel soldiers had stepped from the swarm and heaved their spears. And the spears had flown like rockets and the choppers had exploded and now Todd Jr. stood sick and terrified, gawking at the burning wreckage. There were letters and numbers on the tail section in the tree.

USMC-8912, it read. The characters big and bold. Todd Jr. wondered how many soldiers had just died. He looked at his father, who was gazing impassively at his troops, oblivious to the death and devastation he'd just caused.

It was too much to take in, so Todd Jr. turned one hundred eighty degrees.

The sight that greeted him in this direction made him scream.

Before him, standing perfectly still, was Professor Steele. Or rather, Professor Steele's *body*. Steele's head was gone.

Junior screamed again, turned and ran. He sprinted twenty feet, tripped on a log, and fell face-first into the mud. A strong hand jerked him to his feet. It was his father.

"Watch," said the big man.

Shaking and blubbering, Todd Jr. stood. His eyes found Steele's head. It was resting on a flat rock nearby.

The face was gone, and two Fabrinels were kneeling before the open cavity, cutting into the "brain" with thin lasers, cutting neatly, precisely.

Todd Jr. saw with dumb recognition that the thin beams were coming from the Fabrinels' eyes. The cutting continued, then stopped abruptly.

One of the Fabrinel cutters reached into the brain cavity with needle-tipped tweezers, plucked out a glowing cylinder of liquid and handed it to Todd Sr.

Junior watched as the big man took the cylinder, held it up to the light, and then, with his other hand, removed the medallion from his jacket pocket.

Junior gasped. The medallion was no longer wrapped in silk, but instead encased in a clear envelope of glass. Todd Sr. lifted the relic in its strange sheath and passed the tiny cylinder into it. The cylinder penetrated the glass and the glass went from clear to red.

"What's happening?" asked Junior.

Uhlgoth looked at him. "They will solve the riddle of the medallion before my ship arrives."

"Who will? What riddle?" asked the boy, his curiosity momentarily overruling his fear.

"Steele and the old man will solve the riddle."

Todd Jr. stared at his father. "What? Peeples? The old guy? He's dead. And Professor Steele ..." He glanced at the headless body standing perfectly still; then down at the open skull cavity. "He's ..." Junior again suppressed the urge to vomit.

Finley looked at the medallion. "They're working on the problem now."

Junior remembered how his father had commanded Steele to take the old man's mind, just before Peeples's execution. And how the professor had jabbed his fingers into the old man's eye socket. Now they'd taken the little cylinder from Steele's brain. Todd guessed at what was happening: Peeples and Steele were machines. And now their combined machine intelligence was coursing around the relic, "solving the problem."

"The Mendari scum who befriended the savages long ago," said his father, "gave this … medallion, as you call it, to the savages' leader. Their chief." He held the glass-encased icon up to the sun. "It has special powers."

"It opened the boulder," said Junior.

"The Chamber of the Stars is a trifle compared with the other secret …" Uhlgoth's voice drifted. "A vast treasure. A treasure hidden in one of these valleys. Close at hand."

"Treasure? What kind of treasure?" said Junior.

"Unknown," said Uhlgoth, and he stared at Junior with wide, unblinking eyes. "I tortured a Mendari prisoner for days to learn the answer to that question." He looked away and his jaw tightened. "But he would not talk."

Todd Jr. felt nauseated all over again. His father was a murderer. A *torturer*. It was too much to bear.

"No matter," said Uhlgoth, re-depositing the medallion in his coat. "The riddle will be solved and we will collect the treasure. Just as we will recapture the Earth witch."

He looked at Todd Jr. "My ship is almost here," he said. "When it arrives, just after dark, we will load our spoils and go."

Vistrig, the giant Fabrinel, was projecting another holographic map from his inverted eyeball and Uhlgoth turned and studied it.

"More enemies now, lord," said the giant. "Hatchlings."

Uhlgoth stared at the map and his face twisted with rage.

There were three bright red dots, two ridges away, representing Ina, Thaddeus and Achak. But now there were also fifty to sixty faint, barely visible dots near the others.

"They have seeds!" Uhlgoth roared. "They're growing an army to guard the Earth witch."

He turned and faced his fighters. "Prepare to move. Our enemies are not far, but there is a new threat." The swarm hissed and clicked. "We must find and kill them before they strengthen."

The mob clicked in unison.

"Prepare to run!" Uhlgoth cried. "Prepare to fight!"

A group of seven enormous Fabrinels pushed through the crowd and knelt before Uhlgoth. "Shall we fight, lord?" asked the leader.

Todd Jr. stared at the group in awe. The main Fabrinel army, the swarm that had gathered on the road near the utility truck, was a diverse mix of creatures. Large and small, wiry and stout, old and young, some with blank mannequin faces and yellow eyes, some (like Manuel and Roberto) with faces stolen from the people they'd murdered.

This group of seven was different. For one thing, they were all enormous. Each was larger than the largest pro football lineman, with enormous chests, arms and necks. All had blank, Plasticine heads and searing yellow eyes. And all were armed to the teeth. Todd Jr. wondered where they'd been hiding.

His father answered the leader's question. "No, my

friend," he said. "You seven are to stay in back. Stay safe. You are not to fight. Not until I command it. Is that understood?"

"Yes, lord." The group rose as one and retreated into the throng.

"Why don't you want them to fight?" asked Todd Jr.

"They are Eltura," his father replied. "A special breed of Fabrinel. My creation. They were designed and hatched for one purpose: to hold the witch, when the time comes. To hold her and subdue her and keep her alive until she is on the ship."

Vistrig extinguished the topographic map and dropped to one knee so that Todd Jr. could climb onto his back again. The boy hesitated before his father. "Are you still my dad?" he asked quietly.

The question seemed to trouble the big man and he turned to the boy. "Yes," he said thickly. "I am your father. And I am Uhlgoth. We share the same vision. We have become one."

"What vision?"

Todd Sr. gazed through a gap in the trees, back toward the Clement Valley. "A nation," he said slowly. "A world … a galaxy … where nature is controlled. Where there is discipline. Order. Where wildness does not exist. The Goddess is the key."

Uhlgoth raised his fist. "MOVE!" he commanded. And the swarm was underway once again.

Five

"Girl Scouts," said Sean. He was standing on a low tree branch alongside Achak, gazing north along Clearwater Ridge, toward the fire lookout. Binoculars he'd taken from Thaddeus's pack were pressed firmly to his eyes.

Girl Scouts?" said Achak. "What are *Girl Scouts?*"

"You know," said Sean. "Girls. Like, from our grade." He looked at Warren, sitting on the ground next to Mirra. "They do hikes and learn skills and stuff. And, oh yeah, sell cookies. Really good cookies."

Achak looked at him, puzzled.

"Recognize any of them?" asked Warren.

Before Sean could answer, Achak pulled him off the branch and whispered to the group.

"Everybody down," he said. "They're getting close. If we're fortunate, they'll pass right on by."

Peering out through the trees, Warren could see the group clearly now: seven kids and three adults, some with walking sticks; all carrying packs. They were following the ridge-top trail, winding steadily closer through glorious alpine meadow.

Suddenly Warren could hear the group, as well as see it. They were singing. Loudly. Happily. A ridiculous song about a lost meatball.

"Where's Thaddeus?" Sean whispered.

"In the hatchery," said Ina. "Hatchlings are emerging. He had to be there." She peered at the Girl Scouts through the ferns. "If they stick to the trail they won't see him."

They watched the girls approach.

Looking down slope, Warren could see Thaddeus working amid the cylinders, moving carefully from one bizarre stalk to the next, keeping low. The trail passed only one hundred feet uphill from the nursery, but the view was blocked by a jutting promontory of rock. If the scouts stayed on the trail and didn't look back once they'd passed the promontory, they'd never see the nest. If they didn't venture into the forest, they'd never see Warren or the others, either.

Sean slid back in the ferns and tugged on Warren's leg. Warren slid back even with him and Sean whispered in his ear. "Warren; this is our chance to get out of here. We'll run to that group. Scout leaders always carry satellite phones on trips like this. We'll …"

Achak twisted like a snake, lunged silently toward the boys and brought a gleaming knife blade down against Sean's throat. "Be still," he hissed.

Sean's eyes went wide. Both boys froze.

" … On top of spaghetti!
All covered with cheese,
I lost my poor meatball,
When somebody sneezed …"

The silly, happy singing was loud now. The scouts were close, passing between the trees and the promontory. In a few seconds they'd be gone.

"It rolled down the garden,
and under a bush,
and then my poor meatball,
was nothing but mush."

The words rang. It was a fine, clear morning. The meadows were glorious. The surrounding wilderness stunning. The air crisp and clean. Warren understood why the scouts felt like singing.

The group was passing. In a moment …

"Wait!" shouted a girl, and the singing abruptly ceased. "Can I get a picture? Off that point?"

Warren's heart jumped. He knew that voice.

"The sunrise is so beautiful," said the girl. "Just a quick picture?"

"Sure," said the leader. "Anybody else want a picture? Philomena's got a good spot there."

Philomena Phelps! Warren peered carefully through the salal, heart thumping.

Philomena Phelps set down her pack, unzipped a side pouch and began fishing around for a camera. She wore a baseball cap, and her hair was pulled back in a long ponytail. She looked tan and strong.

Ina cursed. "She'll see the hatchery."

"I know that girl," said Warren. "I could …"

"Do it!" hissed Achak. "Make something up. Keep

them off that point. Get rid of them."

Warren nodded and started to rise. Achak pulled him back down. "Be quick," he said.

"Right," said Warren.

He stood and made his way through the undergrowth.

Six

"Hey Phil!" Warren called, striding boldly out of the trees. "Is that you?"

Phil looked up from her pack and smiled a big, startled smile. The other scouts and leaders turned.

"Warren!" she cried. "What are you doing here?"

"Just, um, having breakfast," he said. He waved toward a tiny knoll overlooking the opposite valley. "View's way better from that side. If you want a picture."

"No, but I mean, how did you *get* here?" Phil looked around. "Did you camp here? Are you alone?"

Warren shrugged, and answered in the blandest voice possible. "Alone. Yeah. I like to hike alone sometimes."

Phil regarded him curiously.

"You're Warren Wilkes," said one of the leaders; a tall, fit-looking woman in her mid-forties.

"Yes," said Warren.

"It said in the paper you were doing community service all summer. At that rest home."

"Ridgecrest. Yeah."

The woman glanced at the other adults. "So how come you're here? Didn't you just start that?"

Warren shrugged again. "I needed a break," he said. "Plus, it burned down. So I can't really work there anyway."

Back in the bushes, Ina buried her face in her hands and Achak sighed with disgust.

"Burned down?" said another leader. "Ridgecrest? When?"

"Last night," said Warren, wishing he hadn't mentioned it. "I guess you guys wouldn't know that, since you've been out here. Obviously."

"Ridgecrest burned?" cried one of the girls, bursting into tears. "My grandma lives at Ridgecrest!"

"I think they got everybody out okay," said Warren quickly. "I saw tons of people on the street. I bet your grandma's fine."

"So you saw this fire yourself?" said the forty-something mom, glancing at the other adults as she spoke. "Last night? But now you're here, thirteen miles in?"

"Yeah," said Warren. "I hiked all night."

"Alone?"

"Um. Yeah."

There was a muffled *THUMP*, and the girls and leaders turned to see Thaddeus crouched, cat-like, on the end of the rock promontory, gazing at them coolly.

"Alone," Warren repeated, completely unnerved by Thaddeus's sudden appearance. "And with my, um, cousin there. Um, Ted. Yeah. Big Ted. I forgot about him."

The scouts and leaders stumbled back. Phil (closest to the promontory) forgot about her camera and pack and retreated slowly.

Thaddeus had leapt onto the rock from the slope below, and with his hulking frame, rustic attire and riotously untamed beard and hair, he looked huge and shocking and wild.

Thaddeus opened his mouth as if to address the group, and instead emitted three supersonic, eardrum-punishing clicks. Then he growled in English. "Agents!"

Warren heard Ina and Achak explode from the bushes behind him.

"Soldiers!" Thaddeus cried, removing his huge knife from its sheath. "Split up! Ina, take Mirra to the tower. We …"

"Mirra's gone!" said Ina. "She slipped away."

The scout leaders were dragging the girls away from Warren and his strange companions now as quickly as possible. But Phil was still near the promontory.

"Phil!" snapped the forty-something mom. "Grab your pack and get over here. NOW!"

"FBI!" boomed a voice on a bullhorn. "Drop your weapons and put your hands in the air!"

Warren heard the sudden rumble of helicopters and saw helmeted, rifle-toting soldiers and law-enforcement types swarming toward the group from three sides.

"Hands where we can see 'em!" the voice roared. "NOW!"

Thaddeus dropped his huge hunting knife and lifted his arms. Ina and Achak did the same.

Seven

Soldiers and law enforcement officers were suddenly among them. All around them. Some leveled weapons on Thaddeus, Ina and Achak. Others shoved Warren, Sean and Phil together near the rock promontory. A contingent of US Marshalls and armed park rangers herded the hysterical scouts and their leaders down the trail in the opposite direction.

"MOVE! MOVE! MOVE!" came the sharp, shrill orders for the scouts. "Leave your packs!"

The girls screamed. One of the leaders tried to writhe free. "We've left Phil!" she cried. "She's back there."

"Keep moving!" commanded a ranger. Strong arms pushed, pulled, and dragged the scouts away; kept the group running in a tight knot. "We'll bring her to you. Keep moving!"

On the promontory, Warren studied the forces arrayed

around them: Clement County sheriff's deputies, FBI and ATF agents wearing helmets and bulletproof vests, park rangers and US Army soldiers in fatigues.

Breathing hard, drenched in sweat, they'd been moving fast. Now agents were handcuffing Thaddeus, Ina and Achak. Shouting their rights over the rumble of the helicopters. Shoving them uphill.

The choppers—a large army transport and a small attack ship bristling with guns and missiles—were landing on the far side of the ridge.

"We found the boys," a Clement County deputy near Warren was saying into a satellite phone. "They look fine."

"What's happening, Warren?" Phil asked.

Half a dozen soldiers had formed a ring around the children, facing out. Weapons ready.

"Do you know what this is about?" Phil's voice was surprisingly calm. "What's happening? What did those people do? Your friends, I mean. *Are* they your friends?"

"Yeah," said Warren. "They are. And they didn't do anything bad."

"Just protect his mom," Sean added.

Warren scanned the meadows, hoping to catch a glimpse of Mirra.

"Your mom?" said Phil. She looked at Warren. "Is your mom here?" She paused. "Warren ... I thought your mom was ..."

"It's Diers and Nelson," declared a nearby deputy, interrupting Phil and drawing the children's attention. The deputy was peering through binoculars, studying a spot hundreds of yards down the ridge.

Warren shielded his eyes from the rising sun and saw two walkers approaching fast, weapons and badges glinting in the morning light. He stared, and an inexplicable shiver traveled the length of his spine.

Eight

"Weren't Diers and Nelson at the bucket truck last night?" asked another deputy.

"Yeah, and no word from either of 'em after that," said another. "Found their car on the shoulder but no sign of them."

"Chief'll be glad for some good news," said the first deputy, eyes still glued to his binoculars. "Wonder how they got clear in here, though."

Warren turned and saw Thaddeus, Ina and Achak being hustled toward the crest of the ridge by a throng of soldiers and agents. Warren didn't know about the two helicopters just destroyed at Uhlgoth's hands, two ridges away, but the soldiers and police did. And they were jumpy.

Warren saw Thaddeus, towering over his captors, and wondered why he, Ina and Achak had allowed themselves to be arrested in the first place. Thaddeus could probably fight twenty soldiers by himself, easy.

Maybe they're not bullet proof, Warren thought. *Or maybe they're worried about our safety.*

Diers and Nelson were getting closer. Everyone was watching them now. But sudden shouting drew all eyes down slope.

"They found the hatchery," said Sean.

It was true. Two soldiers and two ATF men were inside Thaddeus's carefully arranged "garden" on the slope below, peering at the bizarre growths, poking at them tentatively. Another was shooting video of the emerging stalks.

"Listen," Warren said, to the soldiers around him. "The plants down there ... tell your guys to be careful with them. They're not regular plants."

The soldiers exchanged glances but gave no reply. Diers and Nelson were two hundred yards away now and deputies were stepping forward to meet them. Thaddeus and the others had disappeared over the ridge.

"Tell them not to hurt the stalks," said Warren, as Phil stared at him. "You don't understand. It's a hatchery. It's a nest."

"Easy, Son," replied a lieutenant, over the rhythmic *THUMP, THUMP, THUMP* of another incoming chopper. "This'll all be straightened out soon enough."

"This one's for the kids," announced an FBI agent wearing mirrored sunglasses, as the new chopper swept into view. "Let's get 'em up to the landing area."

Sean leaned close to Warren as soldiers herded them uphill. "Warren, where's your mom?" he asked.

Warren shook his head, despondent. "I don't know."

Diers and Nelson were fifty yards away now and a Clement County deputy called to them over the roar of the incoming chopper.

"Where you guys been hiding?"

No reply. The two deputies kept coming.

"Why are they looking at *us*?" asked Phil, and Warren saw what she meant. Diers and Nelson were staring at the three of them, adjusting their course as they approached.

The soldiers noticed this, too, and four Army Rangers stopped and leveled weapons at the deputies, as other soldiers shoved the children on.

"Floyd! Leigh!" shouted a Clement County deputy. "What's up, guys? We found your car by that bucket truck mess. We all thought ..." his voice trailed off. "How the hell'd you get here?"

Diers and Nelson ignored him. "Where's the mother?" Diers cried. The helicopter was almost directly overhead now. "I see the boy. Where is the mother?"

Warren felt another chill as he watched the two deputies come. They *looked* like Clement County deputies all right: crisp uniforms, neat haircuts, gleaming badges. But there was something off about the way they walked. The way they held their heads. About the cast of their skin in the morning light.

More soldiers were raising weapons now, even as a tight group continued herding the kids uphill. More FBI and ATF agents were jogging toward the group, and even the team in the hatchery was peering uphill.

"What's happening?" Phil asked. She grabbed Warren's hand as they jogged. "What's wrong?"

"They're not real," he whispered, locking eyes now with Lieutenant Diers.

"They're not real!" Warren screamed. "They're not real deputies! They're machines!"

Phil noticed with alarm that none of the soldiers or agents laughed or even smirked.

"Give us the boy," Lt. Nelson cried. "Give us Warren Wilkes."

"RUN!" screamed a soldier, and suddenly the group was sprinting uphill.

Nine

Strong hands shoved and carried the kids over the rough, uneven ground. The ring of soldiers and cops tightened around them.

They stumbled through a bright, gurgling stream, no more than twelve inches wide.

"Drop your weapons!" a voice behind them cried. And then Warren heard popping sounds, and bullets ricocheting off rocks.

The next few moments unfolded like a terrifying dream. The soldier beside Phil and Sean crashed to the ground, blood gushing from his neck. The children screamed.

"GET DOWN!" the agent behind Warren commanded, and the children dove for the dirt. The agent spun. Opened fire. *BOOM! BOOM! BOOM!* The roar of his handgun was deafening.

Warren rolled in the grass and saw at least ten agents and soldiers firing point-blank at Diers and Nelson now, firing with handguns and automatic rifles, firing a blaze of bullets at the artificial deputies who stood there, bending and twitching and warping and weaving; but never falling. Never falling.

The assault subsided for a millisecond, and in that fleeting breath, Diers and Nelson raised their own guns and returned fire, weapons roaring like dynamite in a mine shaft.

Two more soldiers guarding the kids crashed to the ground and now Diers and Nelson were moving, running headlong into the storm of bullets, firing and then attacking with feet and fists.

Phil and Sean screamed and buried their faces in the grass, but Warren couldn't look away.

Diers and Nelson were getting closer, and soldiers and agents were dying all around.

The arriving helicopter aborted its landing, shot up two hundred feet and banked hard, moving into position over the battle and adding to the cacophony.

Warren saw Diers fly at a soldier, rip the man's automatic rifle out of his hands, rear back and open fire on the roaring, swooping chopper. He opened his mouth and vomited a torrent of clicks. Louder than a cannon.

The helicopter's windshield exploded, the craft's thundering engine seized, flames erupted under the landing skids, and with a shriek, the machine pitched violently to the right and slammed rotor-first into the verdant meadow.

Warren saw the gleaming steel rotor clip the ground. Saw the blade tear into the earth. Saw flames swallow the craft.

A roaring tidal wave of heat knocked Warren flat and chunks of flaming metal whickered past his head.

He looked up, and his blood froze.

Diers and Nelson were striding toward him, through the smoke and the shimmering heat, eyes gleaming.

The soldiers, agents and deputies were dead or wounded or hunkered down out of sight and Sean and Phil lay motionless; dead for all Warren knew.

There was a gun laying at his feet. A rifle. He lifted it, and aimed at the approaching deputies.

The weapon felt strange and heavy and huge in Warren's hands. Nothing like the pellet guns and .22s he and his friends used.

Diers and Nelson were twenty feet away and getting closer. Warren fired.

The butt of the gun slammed like a fist into his shoulder, the weapon roared, and Warren screamed. Bullets blasted the Fabrinel deputies—at this range there was no way Warren could miss—and stopped them in their tracks.

Stopped them, but did not kill them.

Whatever alien material Fabrinel skin was made of, it was hard enough to deflect bullets at close range.

Warren raked the weapon back and forth and up and down, but the Fabrinels only cocked their heads.

CLICK! CLICK! CLICK! The rifle's ammo clip went dry and Warren screamed as the Fabrinels lunged.

Ten

A shadow fell across Diers and Warren heard a rushing sound. He saw the deputy glance up, a millisecond before a refrigerator-sized boulder smashed him into the ground.

With a soft *THUMP*, a bearded giant landed nimbly atop the boulder.

"Thaddeus!" Warren cried.

But the big man never glanced at him. Like some Viking berserker he leapt at Nelson—shrieking, knife drawn—and the battle was on.

Sean and Phil crawled next to Warren to watch. Like the fight in the UPS truck, this battle was savage and lightning fast, with kicks and punches to shatter concrete.

Warren heard shouts and gunfire from beyond the ridge—but there was no time to look. Thaddeus was lunging; diving at Nelson with his knife, as she parried with a mangled M-16.

The tip of Thaddeus's enormous knife was glowing, so bright it shimmered and shone even in the morning light. Thaddeus lunged for Nelson's heart, but she was fast. She twisted to the right and smashed the big man's out-stretched arm with a booming kick. The glowing knife flew from his hand and sliced blade-first into the earth at Warren's feet.

Warren plucked the knife out of the dirt. The tip glowed no longer. He tried to hand it back to Thaddeus but Nelson was a cyclone of kicks and punches. She rained blows on the big man's face.

Then Thaddeus hit back.

A booming left smashed her jaw. A thunderous right slammed her head into the boulder that had crushed Diers, and the massive block cracked in half on the impact. Nelson swooned, but now there were new threats.

Eleven

Rough Fabrinel hands seized Warren by the collar and jerked him into the air.

A thousand yards down slope, Fabrinels flooded out of the forest like rats from a sinking ship. Still more of Uhlgoth's beasts were in the hatchery, smashing the new growths Thaddeus and Achak had planted.

Thaddeus tore away from Lt. Nelson, leapt like a charging rhino over Phil and Sean, and with a burst of electric clicks, tackled the Fabrinel that had grabbed Warren, and smashed its head into the ground with both hands.

Warren writhed, spun, twisted away and bounced to his feet, unscathed.

But now they were surrounded. Warren turned in the dirt and saw that five Fabrinels, including Nelson, were closing in from all sides, ringing Thaddeus like hungry wolves. Now the Blank Frame Thaddeus had tackled was getting to its feet, too; clicking and hissing, spoiling for revenge.

Four of the attackers brandished spears and Warren saw that the spear tips—like the tip of Thaddeus's knife—glowed. White hot. Warren saw fear in the big man's eyes.

"Thaddeus!" Warren screamed, preparing to toss him his knife.

"Wait!" Thaddeus cried. And he flung a small object at Warren's feet through the ring of attackers. "Touch the ..." The words died on his lips as Uhlgoth's soldiers rushed forward to kill him.

Warren snapped the object off the ground, and leapt clear.

The spear-bearers lunged at Thaddeus and he dove for an opening, steamrolling the unarmed Fabrinel and somersaulting into the clear.

The big man spun, ripped a watermelon-sized rock out of the dirt, and shot-putted it at the nearest attacker.

CRACK! The rock smashed into the Fabrinel's outstretched spear and slammed it against the creature's forehead, breaking the weapon in half and knocking the beast back. Thaddeus dived again, rolled, and got to his feet, now brandishing the two halves of the fractured spear.

Uhlgoth's soldiers clicked furiously and spread out, surrounding the mountain man again, more warily this time.

"It's a box," Philomena gasped, observing the object Thaddeus had lobbed at Warren. "Like a little jewel box. Open it."

"Hurry," said Sean.

Warren focused. The box was old, very old, and worn, with a tortoise shell lid polished smooth. It felt heavy in his hand. Warren cracked open the lid and cried out in pain, as white-hot light scorched his eyes.

The box contained a tiny orb, bright as a meteor flaming through the atmosphere. Phil was the first to understand.

"The knife!" she cried. "Touch the knife to the light. Make it like the spears."

Warren understood. The Fabrinels—including Thaddeus—were afraid of the light-tipped weapons. Normal weapons couldn't harm them. Even blazing bullets left no mark. But the light weapons …

"Die!" hissed one of the Fabrinels ringing Thaddeus. The attackers were tight around him now, jabbing and thrusting from all sides as the big man bobbed and danced, deftly parrying every thrust with his two spear halves.

And then he lunged. Instead of waiting for the attack to come to him, Thaddeus attacked. Lurching toward one Blank Frame, he faked to the right, then dove left as the creature thrust its spear and missed. Flipping around, mid-dive, Thaddeus jammed the point of his broken spear up, into the Fabrinel's side. The glowing weapon penetrated the machine's synthetic hide like a needle piercing flesh, but there was no blood. Instead, the Fabrinel began to melt and warp and shrink, like plastic in a fire. The beast shrieked and bellowed, melting and imploding as it flailed.

Instantly, the remaining Fabrinels settled on a new strategy. Three of the four beasts charged Thaddeus, flying at him with new ferocity. The fourth turned, lunged at Warren, and knocked him back—sent him flailing across a chunk of smoking, mangled metal. One of the landing skids from the fallen chopper.

Warren cried out as his shin smacked the hard, hot surface, and the tortoise shell box flew from his hand.

He tried to twist away, but the Blank Frame was there, scooping him up, preparing to leap.

And now Warren howled in agony.

One dangling strap of his pack caught on the jagged metal, and as his captor lifted him, the pack cut savagely into his shoulder.

"Wait!" Warren screamed.

But the Fabrinel gave no ground and offered no chance for him to shed the pack.

Sean read the situation in instant. He'd taken Thaddeus's knife when Warren opened the jewel box, and now he dove, blade outstretched, for the glowing orb. It lay amid the wildflowers like a miniature sun.

Sean touched the orb with the tip of Thaddeus's ancient weapon, then sprang toward the Fabrinel's feet, as Phil jumped clear.

The creature's legs were bent. It was ready to leap. Oblivious to Warren's anguished shrieks, it would bound downhill, severing the boy's shoulder in the process.

Sean stabbed. He drove the fiery blade into the top of the Blank Frame's bare left foot, through the creature's Plasticine skin.

The beast howled like a hurricane. Instantly its strength failed, its arm went limp, and Warren twisted free. Sean and Phil jumped aside as the Blank crumpled and thrashed into the ground.

The noise from the dying machine caused its comrades to glance away from their attack on Thaddeus.

It was all the time the big man needed.

In that eye blink, he whipped the white-hot spear point around in a semicircle, nicking all three remaining Fabrinels as he spun.

For a moment they stood, blinking at the big man in disbelief, blinking at each other. Then they stumbled and shrieked and crashed, disintegrating into the meadow. Nelson was the last to go down, and as she fell, she heaved her spear at Thaddeus with a mournful howl, missing his head by an inch.

Warren staggered to his feet, and watched as the four dying machines turned to mush, puddling on the ground like molten silver. As their death cries faded, other sounds filled the air: an explosion, and muffled shouts from the ridge above. The whine of a helicopter lifting off.

More of Uhlgoth's Fabrinels were streaming up the broad, open slope far below, and the Blank Frames wreaking havoc in the hatchery were smashing the new growths with rocks now, and stabbing the nascent life forms with spears.

Thaddeus's eyes flashed red when he saw this, and with a snarl he scooped up his knife, tipped the molten orb back into its tortoise shell box and sprang downhill, leaping fifty feet in one colossal bound, like a berserk grizzly fired from a cannon.

There was no time for Warren to watch Thaddeus's mad descent, observe the helicopter lifting off, or even to thank Sean for stabbing the Fabrinel and saving his life.

Phil was before him, pale and terrified.

"What is this, Warren?" she whispered "What are those things? They're not people." There was blood on her shirt, pants and shoes. Blood from a soldier who'd died trying to protect her. She was shaking from head to toe.

Warren was shaking, too, but he wanted to comfort Phil. "No," he said softly. "They're not people." He stepped forward but now Phil was backing away, eyeing him with sudden suspicion.

"The Finleys and their lawyer ..." she said slowly, "all that stuff about you in the paper ... I never believed it, but ..."

"Phil ..."

"This isn't Warren's fault," Sean said sharply.

"It's okay," said Warren.

But Phil was still edging away, studying both boys warily now. She teetered, then shimmied sideways like a drunk. Her face was pale.

"You okay?" said Warren.

"Thirsty," she croaked, glaring at both of them, looking simultaneously fragile and defiant. "Just really, really thirsty."

She dropped to her knees at the edge of the glittering stream, cupped her hands, drank long and deeply, and splashed the clear, icy water in her face.

"You're supposed to filter that, you know," said Sean, kneeling beside her. "Even up here. I mean, Giardia and all ..."

Phil came up blinking, wiping her wet face with one forearm. "Giardia?" she snorted. The snort turned to soft laughter. The laughter grew louder and was so spontaneous and infectious that Warren began laughing, too. Sean looked hurt, at first, but then he was laughing, as well. Soon they were all howling.

"There's a war," Phil cried. "Helicopters are crashing. People are dying all over the place. Psycho-freak monsters that look like people, but aren't, are killing everything in sight. And you're worried about *Giardia*?"

The three of them fell into the wildflowers, laughing at the absurdity of it.

After a minute Warren sat up and the others did, too. The color had returned to Phil's face and she was no longer shaking.

"Phil," said Warren. "We should try to find your group. If we can ..." He stopped talking, eyes fixed on something behind Sean and Phil. The others turned to see what he was looking at.

The cracked, refrigerator-sized boulder Thaddeus had used to smash Diers was moving. As they watched, it lifted, teetered, and crashed to one side; revealing the deputy's mangled body in the dirt.

The body twitched.

Twelve

Phil let out a strangled cry and Diers lurched to a sitting position, then got to his feet. His uniform was torn and stained and his limbs were bent at impossible angles. But as they watched, his appendages snapped back into place. Pulverized muscles inflated and flexed and his head swung mechanically around, eyes fixing on Warren. He grinned.

"No one to protect you now, Wilkes," he said, his voice pitch shifting, as his machine brain reset itself. He took a step toward the children.

"What do you want?" Phil cried.

Diers grinned and clicked. "With you?" he hissed. "Nothing."

To Warren's horror, the Fabrinel jerked its service revolver from its holster and aimed at Phil's head. Warren jumped in front of her.

But Diers never fired. Instead, he lurched to the right and crashed downhill under a roaring storm of bullets. Bullets fired from a helicopter.

The children spun and watched the chopper rumble down from the ridge like an angry dragon; hugging the ground and roiling the meadow plants with its hurricane breath. As it passed, as it continued to fire on Diers—sending the man spinning and jerking puppet-like, down-hill—Warren saw the pilot.

It was Ina.

Achak was beside her, and now they were zooming down—beyond Diers—strafing Uhlgoth's charging troops.

The blast from the craft's .50 caliber guns blew Diers one hundred yards downhill. But he was not destroyed. As the chopper shot past, Diers leapt to his feet and sprinted toward a jutting promontory of rock. The same promontory Phil had stopped at to take a picture.

Faster than a cheetah, Diers hit the tip of the promon-tory and sprang into the air, narrowly missing the chop-per's tail rotor and catching the passenger-side landing skid with both hands. The chopper lurched sideways and Diers hung from the skid, like a trapeze artist pausing be-tween maneuvers. Then he began pulling himself up.

Thirteen

"Rocket launcher," said Sean, and Warren followed his gaze.

Far below, near the bottom of the meadow, away from the main body of attackers, men were stepping from the forest. One of them lifted a metal tube to his shoulder.

"Uhlgoth," Warren hissed.

But it wasn't Uhlgoth. It was an Army Ranger. The men were soldiers and FBI agents. They knew about the massacres on the ridge and in the neighboring valley. They'd arrived as the firefight with Diers and Nelson was ending. Watching through binoculars, they'd seen Thaddeus's battle with the Fabrinels, and watched Diers leap hundreds of feet to catch the chopper in midair.

Now—as one of his men spoke urgently into a radio—Army Captain Nicholas Bentz focused his field glasses on the helicopter cockpit and saw Ina at the controls. He watched her strafe Uhlgoth's spear-carrying troops and saw Diers pulling himself up, onto the landing skid as the craft careened forward and down.

"Al Qaeda?" asked a soldier behind him.

Bentz snorted. "Yeah. Al Qaeda from Mars."

The chopper abruptly banked toward Bentz and his men, and Bentz turned to the lieutenant holding the metal tube. "Bring it down," he said.

Warren saw a flash of fire, and a moment later the helicopter detonated in midair.

"No!" Warren screamed, "No!" The craft exploded with a resounding *BOOM! BOOM!* and chunks of flaming metal rained down on the meadow. "No!"

Warren's shock turned to wonder.

Three figures were falling *through* the fireball; falling straight down, two hundred feet to the broad, sloping meadow. The flames went out as the creatures plummeted, and they hit the ground and started running.

"Those people are alive," said Phil, her voice flat and weak. "That's impossible."

"Yeah," said Sean. "What else is new?"

On the slope, Ina and Achak were now battling Diers again as if the explosion and fall had never occurred, and a swarm of other Fabrinels was charging toward them, heaving spears as they came.

Thaddeus killed the last of the Fabrinels raiding the hatchery—glanced uphill to check on the children—then leapt down slope.

Three hundred yards away, Captain Bentz stared at Ina and Achak through binoculars. They looked unscathed. The lieutenant who'd fired the missile gaped. A gray-haired FBI agent stared in mute astonishment, face pale.

Bentz swept his binoculars uphill and saw the bubbling, steaming stalks in the hatchery. Some of the stalks had ruptured, revealing quivering gelatinous shapes. Bentz saw hands and arms poking through some of the gelatin and felt a sudden urge to vomit.

He jerked the lenses downhill. There, on the forest edge, the giant, Vistrig, stood watching the battle, flanked by the enormous Eltura, the unit Uhlgoth was saving for Mirra's capture. In the middle of them all stood Uhlgoth himself. But he wasn't watching the fight. Instead, he was staring at something in his hand. Bentz zoomed in and saw a medallion of flashing gold, inside an envelope of glass.

CLICK. CRACK. SNAP, came Uhlgoth's sudden, supersonic command—echoing like cannon fire over the meadow. His troops instantly abandoned their uphill attack.

Bentz stared. Uhlgoth, for some unknown reason, was calling his army back to the woods.

Diers abruptly quit his battle with Achak and Ina, wheeled and leapt downhill.

Too late.

Thaddeus heaved his glowing knife. The blade turned and flashed like a silver lure in the morning sun and hit Diers in the back of the neck. It pierced his hide, and sent him shrieking and wailing into the ground.

Fourteen

Captain Bentz spoke into a satellite phone. "Yes, sir," he said. "We've got enemy combatants *only*, on the lower slope. Yes, sir. The children are in the upper meadow. Near the ridgeline. There's a good eight hundred meter separation. Yes, sir. I understand, sir."

The gray-haired FBI agent, Harwood, stared as Bentz finished his call and handed the phone to another lieutenant.

"General Wilton," Bentz said.

"He know what we're dealing with here?" asked Harwood. He was sweating heavily.

"Enough to know he wants to bomb it into oblivion," said Bentz.

The captain turned to his men. "Heavy strike coming, guys. Fifteen minutes or less. We'll take a position in the cover—down there." He gestured toward the deep forest at the bottom of the slope. "Help guide the strike. Let's move!"

The unit of half a dozen men complied at once and Harwood turned to Bentz as they hustled through tall grass. "What else did General Wilton say?"

"Homeland Security's closed Highway 20," Bentz replied. "Park Service and National Guard's evacuating everybody in a hundred mile swath. Towns, campgrounds, lodges. They're telling the media it's a chemical spill. The big guns in DC are looking at satellite data, the president's being briefed. RCMP's mobilizing across the border."

The FBI agent was staring at text messages on his own phone. "But he doesn't know the nature of the threat?"

"Not a clue."

"Wonderful," said Harwood. "Neither do my guys."

Fifteen

Warren felt dread, not relief, as he watched Uhlgoth's troops drain from the lower slopes of the meadow like a receding tide.

"He got Mirra," Warren gasped. "Uhlgoth got her. There's no other explanation."

Phil looked inquiringly from Warren to Sean.

"Mirra is his mom," Sean explained softly. "The guys down there ... the ones who were attacking ... they want to capture her. Warren, too, if they can. Warren thinks they already have her."

Phil nodded. There were shining tears in Warren's eyes, and he didn't try to conceal them.

"When did you see her last?" Phil asked gently.

"She was hiding in the forest with us when your group came along," he replied, brushing his tears away. "She was there, and then the raid happened. I never saw her after that."

Warren stared at the hatchery. Ina, Achak and Thaddeus had regrouped there and were scanning the surrounding meadows and slopes. "Uhlgoth got her," Warren repeated miserably, "he must have."

He was wrong.

In fact, Mirra had crept away just before the soldiers arrived and the chaos erupted. Ina's probing questions: *"Why have you been living at Ridgecrest? Why don't you have a family? Why don't you have a life?"* riled her. And the story about the Ridgecrest arson, and the kidnapping, and Peeples's role in it all—had shaken her to the core. Lying in the brush, waiting for the Girl Scouts to pass, she couldn't breathe.

And so, as everyone watched the scouts and listened to their ridiculous song, Mirra crept through the forest in the opposite direction. She crawled at first, then jogged. Exiting the small grove of trees, she ran quickly up and over the crest of the ridge, and stood gazing at the vistas on the far side.

The fog had almost disappeared from over here, and the views were thrilling. Wild. Pulse-quickening.

Mirra soaked it all in: rolling alpine meadows, lush flowers, iridescent insects, and deep emerald forests far below.

A stream tumbled through the meadow; the air was bitingly clean and fresh, and the sun soothed her shoulders like a slow massage.

Mirra shoved aside the surreal events of the morning: the alarming revelations, the sudden earthquake. Shoved it all aside and let the beauty of the day overwhelm her.

She'd face reality in a minute, she told herself.

But the next thing she knew she was running through the meadow, laughing and leaping like a child. She'd meant to go straight back to Ina and the others. She'd only wanted to get away for a moment, to think and clear her head.

The moment proved too much to resist. Soon she was running with joyful abandon. Running along the crest of the ridge. Running toward … what? She'd never been to this place before. She was certain of that. Certain …

And yet …

There was something about the rise ahead … something about the way the meadow rolled to a distinctive knob, that seemed familiar. There was something on the other side of that knob; something she knew about in her muscles and bones, but couldn't recall in her mind.

She had to see what was on the other side.

Sixteen

Uhlgoth's freakish mob clogged the forest around him, clicking and hissing softly. Todd Jr. was there, too: shaky and pale and half-starved, looking up at his father like a whipped mongrel.

Uhlgoth's sentries had seen no sign of Mirra near Thaddeus, Ina or Achak, and Uhlgoth had ordered an abrupt cease-fire.

"Where is she?" he growled, the words crashing from his mouth like falling slabs of stone. "Where is the Earth witch?"

"Not far, lord," said Vistrig, once more projecting the holographic map from his inverted eyeball. "Two miles down ridge."

Uhlgoth scowled. "She travels alone?"

"Yes, lord."

"Toward the tower?" Uhlgoth's voice quivered uncharacteristically, and Todd Jr. thought he sounded vulnerable, even … afraid.

"Yes, lord," Vistrig replied. "Two park rangers are observing her."

Todd Jr. strained his ears. He could hear a faint, static-riddled radio transmission playing inside Vistrig's topographic map.

"The rangers don't know who she is," Vistrig said. "They think she's a hiker, and they have orders to evacuate the area. They're moving toward her now."

"It's some kind of trick," grumbled Uhlgoth, practically spitting the words. He pointed up slope, toward Thaddeus and the others. "They've diverted us here while the witch is regaining her identity. Reclaiming her power."

"It's possible, lord," said Vistrig. The neon blue map streaming from his eyes flickered and grew brighter.

"But the witch's movements indicate that she has not yet achieved self-awareness. She *will* remember who she is. But it has not happened yet."

"But what about the earthquake? The wind last night?"

"She's waking up, lord," Vistrig replied. "But she is not yet fully awake. Not yet in control."

Uhlgoth was still skeptical. He glanced uphill, toward the hatchery. "What about the Guardians? Why do they linger here? Why leave the witch unprotected?"

Vistrig paused, and scanned reams of cascading data inside the hologram.

He looked up suddenly. "They don't know where she is," he said.

The news shocked Uhlgoth. But his surprised expression quickly gave way to a cruel smirk.

Vistrig said, "She wandered away before the fighting

began, lord. To confront her demons."

Uhlgoth had heard enough. With a sharp *CLICK! CLICK! CRACK!* he summoned a small Blank Frame from the crowd. The creature waded toward him, then knelt, yellow eyes glowing like tiny lanterns.

"Drink this," said Uhlgoth, and Todd Jr. saw that his father held the little vile of blood Peeples had given him—blood the old man had stolen from the Ridgecrest clinic.

"Yes, lord," said the Blank.

Junior watched in disgust as the Blank took the crimson vile and downed the blood in one slurping gulp.

"That's sickening," said Junior. But no one seemed to hear.

Within fifteen seconds, the Fabrinel began to change: skin darkened, limbs lengthened, hips widened, curves appeared. Thick dark hair sprang from the creature's Plasticine head and its face softened and morphed into a visage of strength and beauty. The eyes changed last; like clear vessels filling with liquid. Tranquil green replacing putrid yellow.

Then it was done. And Todd Jr. found himself staring at a near perfect replica of Mirra, or Onatah. As the metamorphosis concluded, the fake lifted her head and smiled a brilliant, beguiling smile.

"You've made a copy of the woman you're trying to capture?" whimpered Todd Jr. "Why?"

Uhlgoth answered as he circled his new creation, inspecting her closely. "The Guardians have lost their beloved Goddess," he said mockingly. "We will send her back into their caring embrace."

Another Fabrinel knelt before Uhlgoth and presented

him with a small rectangular case. Uhlgoth took the case, opened it, and removed a gleaming silver dagger the size of a letter opener. It was tipped with blinding white cyber toxin: a tiny pinpoint of shockingly bright radiation that lit up the forest and the ghoulish faces huddled fifty deep in all directions. Todd Jr. moaned in pain and shut his eyes tight, but the searing pinpoint lingered in his head like a camera flash.

Junior buried his face in his hands, wishing for the thousandth time that he was home. When he finally opened his eyes again, his father was handing the dagger to the fake Mirra.

"The three Guardians are wary," said Uhlgoth. "Clever. But you will deceive them. You will slay them all."

Seventeen

One thousand yards up-slope from Uhlgoth and his army, things were happening in the hatchery.

"Onatah has not been captured," said Achak, staring at his three-dimensional shell map as Phil watched in wonder.

The neon blue hologram twinkled like a Christmas ornament in the morning light. "She's moving toward the tower," said Achak, "except ..."

"Except what?" said Warren.

"She's turning," said Achak. He glanced at Thaddeus. "Toward the pictures."

"What pictures?" asked Warren.

Warren could see Ina out of the corner of his eye, moving quickly around the upper slope. She was carrying fallen soldiers and law enforcement officers to a grassy, protected area under an outcropping of rock. Most of the dead were bloody and mutilated and Ina had asked the children not to watch. Warren tried to focus on Achak and his hologram.

"What pictures?" Warren asked again.

"She's remembering," said Thaddeus.

Achak nodded.

"What *pictures*?" demanded Warren.

"Petroglyphs," murmured Achak.

"Stone pictures," said Thaddeus. "Very old." He looked at Warren. "The petroglyphs are off the trail. Not marked. Your mother wouldn't go there unless her memory was coming back."

The mountain man was on his knees in front of one of the bubbling, steaming, barrel-sized stalks a few paces away.

As the children watched, he found a crack in the side of the stalk, inserted his hands, and ripped the fibrous casing open, splitting the barrel cleanly apart. Steaming liquid gushed from the ruptured stalk and a brown, sticky-wet hatchling sloshed onto the ground, thrashing violently. Phil covered her mouth with her hand and stifled a scream.

"It's a hopeful sign that she's gone to the pictures," Thaddeus continued nonchalantly, utterly unfazed by the viscous brown blob undulating at his feet. "Hopeful indeed."

Phil teetered as she watched the bizarre blob. Her face was pale.

Achak looked up from his map. "Park rangers are watching Onatah," he said. "They're moving toward her now."

Thaddeus grunted. "I'll go," he said, and he sprang to

his feet. The brown blob continued to writhe and inflate in front of his boots. More stalks were rupturing now, and more wet, wiggling shapes were flopping and sloshing onto the soft meadow plants. It was such a freakish, unsettling sight that the children couldn't turn away.

Ina called to Thaddeus from outside the hatchery.

"Yes," she said. "Go. Help Onatah get to the tower." She glanced at Achak. "We will hold Uhlgoth as long as we can."

Thaddeus strode from the hatchery, sheathing his broad knife as he walked. "You're coming with me," he said flatly, stepping in front of the children and glancing from face to face. "But first Warren must tell his troops what to do."

"My what?" said Warren. And then a vague memory from the previous night floated back into his head. Thaddeus had asked him to touch the seeds. Had said he'd be "like a general."

"Speak to the hatchlings now," said Thaddeus. "Command them. They will obey no other."

"But, um ..." said Warren, and he realized suddenly that Phil and Sean were staring at him.

He felt his cheeks redden but set back his shoulders and turned to face the hatchlings as if he knew what he was doing. In reality, he had no clue. The adults were watching now, too.

Warren surveyed the hatchery. The little patch of meadow had become a surreal garden inhabited by pulsing, rupturing stalks. Eight of the stalks were dead—smashed by Uhlgoth's minions before Thaddeus stopped them. These sat withering and desiccating in the sun.

But the rest of the garden was clearly alive. All around,

softly humming cocoons were splitting; hemorrhaging fresh organisms onto the delicate meadow plants. The mucus-coated hatchlings changed fast.

Immediately after bursting from the stalks, the nascent Fabrinels writhed wildly, twisting and jerking out of fetal position; stretching and inflating in the warm morning sun. There were pale, hairless, Plasticine bodies with yellow eyes, and heavy-set brown bodies; like the brown blob Thaddeus had helped moments earlier.

Unlike the Plasticine versions, the brown forms were covered with dense fur. Upon emergence, the fur was wet and flat, but as the creatures expanded, the fur dried and rippled in the breeze.

The amorphous blob Thaddeus had helped was quickly taking shape. It had a massive head and four muscular limbs.

As they watched, it rolled onto all fours and arched its back. Limbs swelled. Great, curving claws burst from padded feet. A massive hump appeared between the beast's shoulder blades.

Sean moaned in terror as the creature swung its great head toward them, woofed twice, and fixed its eyes on Warren: small, black, intelligent eyes.

"It's a brown bear," said Phil, in a quiet, incredulous voice. "I've seen them in Alaska."

"Yeah," said Warren, and he counted twelve other bears in various stages of birth and expansion. There were at least two dozen humanesque Fabrinels, as well.

All of the creatures—*all* of them—were staring at him.

"Thaddeus," he said weakly, without ever taking his eyes from the hatchlings. "What am I supposed to say?"

Thaddeus glanced at Ina. "You can command them to

take orders from the three of us. That's probably the easiest thing."

"Um, okay. Sure." Warren was relieved, but also vaguely disappointed. He took a step forward.

"Hello men," he said, trying to sound commanding. As soon as the words were out of his mouth, he remembered that not all of the Fabrinels were male. That was obvious.

"I mean, hello *people*," he said, recalling just then that at least half of the Fabrinels were bears.

"I mean, um, creatures … Things."

He stammered. Phil laughed softly behind him and Thaddeus rolled his eyes.

"Lad …" said Thaddeus, but Achak—who was still monitoring his hologram map—interrupted.

"Aircraft approaching," he said. "Heavy armaments."

Thaddeus placed one huge hand on Warren's shoulder. "Command them, lad. Now!"

"Listen up!" Warren shouted. All of the Fabrinels stared at him. The wiggling newborns stopped wiggling and peered at him through their glistening viscous membranes.

"We're in the middle of a battle. I'm sorry you had to be born today."

"Get on with it!" Thaddeus cried.

"You are to take orders from Thaddeus or Ina or Achak!" Warren shouted. "Listen to them. Do what they say."

"Thank you," said Thaddeus. And he began clicking like a machine gun.

Instantly, five bears and eight humanesque Fabrinels were on their feet, stepping to two spindly tree-like structures that had sprung from bubbling stalks of their own.

Warren had seen the "trees" earlier but hadn't compre-hended their purpose. Now, as he stared, he understood.

The "trees" held weapons. Freshly made weapons: spears. Tomahawks. Bows. Quivers full of arrows.

He remembered the little bags he'd taken from the chamber of light. A couple of the bags had been decorat-ed with pictures of weapons. Thaddeus and Achak had planted the seeds and the weapon trees had grown out of the ground just like the Fabrinels.

As Warren watched, the humanesque Fabrinels snapped weapons off the trees and sprinted toward Thad-deus. The hulking bears had already galloped to his side.

"Let's move!" Thaddeus cried.

Warren hugged Ina as he passed her. "Good luck," he said. It was a spontaneous gesture, and Ina seemed touched by it.

"Find your mother," she replied. "Help her."

With that, Warren and the other children found them-selves running along Clearwater Ridge in the strangest company imaginable.

Eighteen

In the trees below, Vistrig had discovered the approaching jets inside his hologram. Uhlgoth and Todd Jr. stared at the twinkling, ever changing map as Vistrig narrated.

"Enemy aircraft, lord. Two fighter jets. Heavily armed."

"Their target?" asked Uhlgoth.

"Us," Vistrig replied, and Junior's heart froze. "They have orders to avoid the hatchery. Because of the children."

Uhlgoth gazed uphill.

"They will drop their bombs here," said Vistrig. He hesitated; stood motionless, as he scanned the ocean of data inside his map. "High explosives. Substantial damage to our forces likely."

"When?" asked Uhlgoth.

"Three minutes, thirteen seconds."

Todd Jr. wanted to bolt through the trees, but he didn't have the strength. And now his father was shrieking again. *CLICK! TOCK! HISS! POP!* The boy wondered how the man could even produce such horrendous, utterly inhuman noises. *CLICK! CRACK! HISS! TOCK!* The sounds were cold and sharp and hard, like shrieks from an assembly-line robot.

Within seconds, the Eltura—the special unit of seven giant Fabrinels—had plowed its way through the crowd and was kneeling at Uhlgoth's feet.

"Run now," Uhlgoth commanded them. "Capture the Earth witch."

"Yes, lord," said the leader, a beast with a massive, ugly head and a neck as thick as a fire hydrant.

"Capture her. Keep her safe until I arrive."

Todd Jr. gasped as Vistrig projected a life-size three dimensional image of Warren Wilkes in front of the Eltura.

"This is the Earth witch's mongrel son," said Uhlgoth. "Capture him also. He may be of value. Destroy all others."

With a burst of staccato clicks, the Eltura wheeled and charged through the assemblage, sprinting toward the open slope with astonishing speed.

"Two minutes, thirty seconds, master," said Vistrig, who was now projecting a crisp image of the two approaching fighter jets.

"Divert them," said Uhlgoth, his voice cold and cruel.

"Yes, lord." Vistrig's holographic projection snapped off and the giant went as rigid as a statute.

Junior stared as Vistrig's right eyeball rolled (like the left one), revealing similar vertical slits. Lasers fired from both eyes and parallel 3-D projections burst to life in front of the giant. These projections weren't maps, but holographic replicas of fighter jet cockpits, complete with gauges, dials and controls. Now Todd Jr. could hear jet noise and bursts of pilot chatter.

"Fly them into the ground," said Uhlgoth.

"Huh?" Junior rasped. "No. Dad! You can't do that!"

"Into the hatchery," said his father.

"Dad! No! Please! Don't kill them!" Junior pleaded and pulled at his father's arm, but Uhlgoth paid no heed.

Vistrig seized control of the jets and the pilot chatter went from calm, to confused, to alarmed.

Todd Jr. heard a low rumble. It built steadily. He'd been to enough air shows to know what it meant. The jets were coming, low and fast.

Vistrig's twin holograms flickered, then stabilized, and the giant cocked his head. "One of the Guardians is competing for control, lord," he reported calmly.

Todd Jr. didn't know what Vistrig meant but apparently his father did because he was once again shrieking at his troops.

"Attack!" Uhlgoth roared. "Rain spears and arrows on the hatchery! Destroy them!"

Half of Uhlgoth's force sprinted from the forest and rushed uphill as the thunder of the jets grew louder.

"The Guardian can't fight and fly jets at the same time," Uhlgoth said to Todd Jr. "This is where we break them."

On the ridge, Ina was projecting two F-16 cockpit

simulations of her own. Like Vistrig, she stood statute-still, eyeballs inverted as Achak and the hatchlings watched.

Achak saw waterfalls of glowing data inside the holograms, sheets of numbers and symbols falling faster and faster as Ina made millions of calculations per second.

"Vistrig's too strong," she said suddenly. "There isn't time."

"Ina," Achak said gently, "make the pilots eject. Let the jets crash against the mountains."

"Vistrig has locked that function," she replied. "He wants to kill them. And us."

The fighter jets roared over the ridge then, steel and glass bullets loaded with high explosives. The ground shook, but the jets were already gone, rocketing forward, banking hard to the south in perfect formation.

"He'll bring them around now and drill them into the hatchery," Ina said flatly. "I can't stop him."

"Yes, you can!" Achak cried. "Fight him!"

Looking downhill, he saw Uhlgoth's troops scurrying from the forest, weapons ready.

CLICK! SNAP! CLICK! Achak shrieked, mustering the remaining Blank Frames. They turned to him with sleepy eyes—skin and fur still wet. They were newborns. Not ready to fight. They needed to sit motionless in the bright sun for several hours. Needed to charge and strengthen.

Achak knew this. Uhlgoth knew it, too.

Achak turned to Ina and gripped her hand. "My sister," he said.

"My brother," she whispered, never turning, never losing focus on the bright, constantly-changing holograms.

Achak turned to find the hatchlings staring at him expectantly. On the slope below, Uhlgoth's surging troops were almost within firing range. In moments they would unleash a shower of toxin-tipped spears and arrows. Ina was defenseless in her present state. She would die, as would the hatchlings still emerging from cocoons. Achak couldn't let that happen.

"For Onatah!" he cried, as he ripped a bow and full quiver of arrows from one of the weapon trees.

"For Onatah!" the hatchlings screamed, as they flexed their new muscles and prepared for the charge.

"ATTACK!"

Achak sprang from the hatchery, surrounded by great, lumbering bears and sleek Plasticine Blanks clutching spears and tomahawks.

Nineteen

Two miles away, Mirra stood in the shadow of a great rock outcropping and gazed up at a smooth, garage-door-sized wall of stone. The wall was decorated with pictures. Intricate pictures. Pictures painstakingly chiseled into the rock ages earlier. Wind and rain and snow and relentless summer sun had aged the pictures and caused their once vibrant colors to soften and fade. But Mirra fell to her knees anyway. There was magic here, a power and energy she could feel as keenly as the breeze caressing her cheek.

She gazed up at the wall in wonder. She had not stumbled on this place by accident. The wall had summoned her.

She extended her right hand and touched the cool stone, struggling to understand the mystery.

She'd been jogging along the main ridge trail, toward

the fire lookout, when an image had blossomed, bright and strange, inside her skull. She veered cross-country after that, not knowing the way to the wall; yet knowing.

There were no signs marking this route. No stakes or cairns. The Park Service had intentionally downplayed the existence of the petroglyphs for decades, fearing vandalism. As a result, few people knew the place.

But Mirra knew. Somehow she knew. Despite what she'd told Ina and Warren, she'd been here before.

Twenty

The faded pictures were arranged in a great circle, and now Mirra got to her feet and gazed at them one by one.

There was the sun, with its stabbing rays. The moon. Stars. Twins. Water birds. A flute player. A hand.

The F-16s rocketed over the ridge, low and fast, but Mirra didn't hear them. She was touching the wall now. Remembering.

"I was here," she whispered, so softly that no one else could've heard. Her knees felt suddenly weak and her eyes welled with tears. "I was here."

She took a breath, then shut her eyes and saw the stone pictures as they once had been: bright and precise and colorful. Mirra leaned closer to the stone and in her mind's eye watched a procession moving along the ridge. A procession of Denelai people. *First People*. Old and

young, male and female, on a warm summer day, ages earlier.

She—Mirra—was in the center of the procession and
little children were holding her hands, looking at her with
bright, smiling faces. They loved her. Adored her. And
she felt the same about them.

Mirra smiled as she remembered the reason for the
procession: the Denelai wanted to show her their magnifi-
cent pictures. They were so eager for her to see what they
had made!

Mirra opened her eyes and saw the wall in its present
state.

Wind whistled over the stone. Some of the pictures
had eroded so much they were nearly invisible. She stared.
"What happened to you?" she whispered. "Where did you
go?"

Dark memories rose in Mirra's mind like monsters
from a well, and she pulled sharply away from the wall.
The ground shook violently and loose rocks clattered off
the outcropping above. Mirra cried out and reached for
the wall again.

A more recent memory burst to mind this time: she
was standing at the wall with a man. A strong, handsome
man with rough hands and kind eyes. He was big, but
gentle. He made her laugh.

"Eric," Mirra whispered, and feelings of loss enveloped her like a slow avalanche.

The tears flowed. She had loved this man, loved him as
she'd never loved anyone before. Where he now?
Panic pulsed through her bones like an electric shock.
This memory was recent. *What became of him?*

"No!" she cried, as images long suppressed flooded

her mind. "I let you die!"

The world went silent then—utterly silent—as if the air had been sucked from the ridge, as if the ridge itself was waiting to see what would happen next. Mirra steadied herself and thought back to a particular moment at the wall.

The memory was bright, vivid, and so real she could almost feel Eric standing beside her. In the memory, he was blowing dust from one of the faded pictographs, gently brushing the image with his bandanna. He stepped back from the wall and laughed.

"Damn," he said. "It looks like you."

He was staring at a pictograph in the center of the great ring of images; a picture of a beautiful woman with long, flowing hair. Eric was right. It did look like her.

It looked like her, because it *was* her.

"That's funny," she replied. "It sorta does, doesn't it."

Mirra snapped back to the present. The ridge was quiet, waiting.

"I never told you who I was," she said, voice choked, grief swelling inside her. "That's why you died. You had no idea what was coming, no way to defend yourself."

Mirra slid back into the bright memory one final time. In the memory, Eric turned and she saw that he was wearing a backpack—a child carrier. There was a baby in the pack. The baby smiled when he looked her way.

The memory evaporated, and Mirra staggered from the wall, struggling to breathe, to collect her wits. It was all coming back to her now—all at once.

A man and woman were jogging down the slope toward her, shouting angrily, as if they'd been trying to get her attention for a long time. Mirra turned and stared at them through tear-stained eyes.

They were National Park Rangers. Drenched in sweat. Frightened.

"Lady," the man gasped. "You gotta get out of here. Come with us. Now!"

Mirra stepped back. "No," she said flatly.

"Lady!" the ranger yelled. "It's not up for debate! We're taking you out. Now!"

"No!" Mirra thundered, and the ridge shook. "I have to find my son."

Twenty-one

Achak careened down from the hatchery—flanked left and right by newborn Fabrinels—straight for Uhlgoth's charging troops.

"For Onatah!" he roared, leaping like a mountain lion, loosing arrow after arrow as he came.

Achak was lithe and fast, and no matter which way he spun or dove or jumped, his toxin-tipped arrows found their mark.

But Uhlgoth's force was huge, and his warriors were fully charged and battle hardened. They were raining spears and arrows on Achak's force, and the newborns were dying in abundance.

A glowing spear whistled past Achak's head and an enormous newborn bear crashed to the ground behind him, shrieking like a jet engine as it withered and died.

Achak knew there was no turning back, no regrouping

or refocusing the attack. He was leading his small force to almost certain annihilation, but there was no alternative. The F-16s were turning, banking hard on the horizon.

Achak saw the jets flash like signal mirrors beyond the far ridge. In seconds they would swing around and leap toward the meadow, augur into the hatchery and kill Ina, the remaining newborns and the pilots in a stupendous fireball.

Achak's desperate goal was to smash through the wave of attackers and kill whoever was controlling the F-16s. Of course, he had another desire as well: to kill Uhlgoth himself.

Achak was a Denelai warrior. He'd witnessed Uhlgoth's savage attack four and a half centuries earlier. Watched his family and friends die and seen his village flattened. Time had not diminished his rage. And now that he was so close to his ancient enemy, it was difficult to keep his fury in check.

"I'm sorry," rumbled a deep-voiced Fabrinel just to Achak's left, as a molten arrow sliced through its plasticine abdomen. The newborn careened left, breaking apart as it crashed to the ground amid jagged piles of loose scree.

Achak glanced up and saw that the jets had finished their turn.

Like a panther, he sprang from an uneven platform of rock, vaulted twenty feet into the air and plucked a whistling spear hurled from below, out of the sky. He crashed to the ground in the thick of Uhlgoth's charging infantry, lowered his bow, whipped the spear around one-handed and rammed it into the throat of an enormous square-headed Blank Frame.

The creature's eyes went wide. It writhed and jerked as it fell, tearing frantically at the ground.

Uhlgoth's surging troops spun to confront Achak, but he was already gone, shooting forward with the spear once again loose and ready in his right hand, the bow in his left.

He could see shapes just inside the trees below, and now an electric blue halo; crisp against the wall of green. It was Vistrig's hologram of the F-16s.

Three enemy Fabrinels exploded from the rocks just ahead and Achak shot to the right, dodging a glowing tomahawk by half an inch.

Achak heaved his spear at the nearest offender and charged recklessly on.

Out of the corner of his eye, he saw one of his new-born bears thrashing wildly amid a swarm of Uhlgoth's troops—its thick coat bristling with glowing spears and arrows. The bear roared and bellowed in agony, and Achak felt sick. But there was no time to reconsider his plan. The jets were almost upon them.

Without slowing, without taking his eyes off the neon blue target a hundred yards below, Achak raised his bow and plucked his last arrow from the quiver on his back.

He could see Vistrig now, standing rigid as a gatepost, streams of laser light flowing from both eyes, the cockpit holograms twinkling and changing before his oddly serene face.

Achak fitted his last arrow to his bow string. Vistrig was enormous. An easy target. One more bound and Achak would fire.

A child clambered onto a stump in front of Vistrig and stood up straight, blocking Achak's line of fire. The boy turned toward him. It was Todd Jr., and there was terror in his eyes. Uhlgoth was there, as well; in the shadows to the boy's left, face twisted in a cruel, mocking sneer.

A dozen Fabrinels exploded from the undergrowth all around, and Achak understood.

It was a trap.

Twenty-two

Uhlgoth had allowed him to penetrate his front lines, and had placed Vistrig in a clearing to draw him in. At the last moment, Uhlgoth had forced his own son onto the stump between Achak and Vistrig, knowing that Achak would not kill a child.

Glowing spears and arrows flashed at Achak from all sides, and the old warrior felt a spasm of rage and sorrow and regret.

He'd failed. He was going to die. Worse yet, his sister, the remaining hatchlings and the F-16 pilots would die, as well. His wild, reckless attack had accomplished nothing, and in a moment, only Thaddeus would remain to defend Onatah.

He'd failed. Unless …

Achak dropped his bow, lowered his head, and rammed the Fabrinel in front of him, blasting the creature forward.

An arrow sliced into Achak's thigh, and his leg melted beneath him. A spear hit him in the back, but his speed and momentum propelled him on.

With a final burst of explosive power, Achak launched the flailing Fabrinel toward the stump. The creature smacked into Junior like a sack of cement and swept the boy into the brush.

Vistrig was in the clear once more.

Achak crashed to the ground at Uhlgoth's feet, twisted his disintegrating torso around in the dirt and slid his bone-handled knife from its sheath. His strength was almost gone. His body was fragmenting. His mind was going dark.

With his last ounce of energy, Achak heaved the glowing knife at Vistrig. He saw the ancient weapon flash as it flew, end-over-end. Saw it wheel straight through the neon blue hologram, and saw it slice, point first into Vistrig's neck.

Achak saw Uhlgoth's sneer vanish and heard him howl with rage. His vision blurred, and he smiled, as the world went dark.

The F-16s passed directly overhead then, shaking the earth; booming like thunder. In two seconds they would slam into the hatchery and detonate.

Ina felt Vistrig relinquish control, and seized it. She released the F-16s' bombs directly over Uhlgoth's charging army. Then forced the jets up. Up.

The bombs detonated. The meadows shook. Locked in formation, the jets screamed over Ina like a hurricane, and cleared the ridge by fifty feet.

Ina knew in her bones that Achak was dead, but she

couldn't consider it. Not yet. Vistrig had damaged the jets. They were going to crash. Ina steered them toward a distant mountain peak.

CRACK! CRACK! The pilots ejected, rocketing clear of their doomed craft. Ina saw parachutes billow a mile beyond the ridgeline. Seconds later, the jets slammed into the distant peak, detonating with a hollow *BOOM! BOOM!*

A low, prolonged rumble followed, as millions of tons of rock and ice avalanched into the valley below.

Ina staggered. The bright cockpit holograms snapped off, her eyes rolled back to normal position, and grief swallowed her like a rolling wave. Her brother was dead. Uhlgoth had killed him.

She collapsed to a sitting position and saw two dozen new hatchlings drying in the sun. They were staring at her, waiting for her command.

She couldn't speak. Her body felt numb. *Frozen.* Ina was a machine, but human emotions and memories lived on inside of her.

She wept. *Achak is gone.*

But he had not died in vain. *No.*

"Let's move!" she cried, standing once more. Her voice was choked and broken, but her thoughts were steady. She would not squander Achak's gift. Uhlgoth's army would regroup and attack again within minutes. There was no time to waste.

"To the tower!" she screamed. "Follow me."

Twenty-three

The two National Park Rangers hustled Mirra cross-country, through expansive, rolling meadow, away from the petroglyphs and toward the main ridge trail. The younger ranger—a fit, twenty-something woman named Abigail—led Mirra by the arm as her colleague spoke frantically into a radio.

They'd heard the rumble of bombs hitting the meadow two miles away, and seen the F-16s smash into the far mountain peak. Now they ran.

"Let me go!" Mirra cried, twisting away. "My son is back there. I have to find him. Let me go!"

"We can't do that," gasped the ranger. "We have orders to clear the area. No exceptions."

"You don't understand," Mirra cried. "My son …"

"Your son will be fine," Abigail lied. "We have other patrols. He'll be fine."

"Schafer, this is Martin!" yelled the ranger with the radio; a tall, balding man with intense blue eyes and a handsome, weathered face. He was used to smiling and chatting with park visitors, but he wasn't smiling now.

"There's a war going on up here. What's the status of that helicopter?"

They all heard a sudden, soft *WHUMP!* close behind and turned in the dirt.

It was Thaddeus, knees bent, dust rising around his feet. Where he'd fallen from was impossible to say. The rangers gaped and Martin forgot about his call—despite the shouted questions coming from the handset.

Thaddeus nodded toward Mirra. "Leave her," he growled. He looked like a giant Old West statue come to life.

"Who the hell are you?" croaked senior ranger Martin. He drew his sidearm and backed off a couple steps.

"No time for that," rumbled Thaddeus. "Leave her and run for your lives."

"We're evacuating the park," said Abigail.

"A fine idea," said Thaddeus. "I'm certain *that* lot would love to make your acquaintance." He tilted his head down-slope and Mirra and the rangers followed his gaze.

Uhlgoth's special Eltura unit was charging uphill in perfect "V" formation, with the largest Blank Frame front and center. Their weapons glinted in the sun, dust hung in the air behind them, and even at this distance their tremendous speed was evident.

The stunned rangers turned back to see Thaddeus scoop a cantaloupe-sized rock off the ground, rear back, and lunge like a Major League pitcher. The rock flashed toward the Eltura like a cannonball, straight and fast and impossibly far.

THWICK! came the faraway sound, as the rock smashed one of the Eltura in the head.

The "V" formation wobbled, then roared forward again, faster than ever. The stunned rangers heard a cacophony of distant, angry *CLICKS* and *POPS*.And now a silver spear was whizzing toward them, slicing through the blue like a Stinger Missile.

"Get down!" Thaddeus cried. He grabbed Mirra and dove with her into the soft meadow plants.

The spear hit the ground fifty feet away and detonated with a *BOOM!*

A hot shockwave slapped the rangers, and the meadow where the spear had landed burst into flame.

Thaddeus leapt to his feet and pulled the rangers up with him. "Run," he said, "or die."

With final, terrified glances at Mirra and Thaddeus, the rangers turned, and practically crashed into Warren, Sean and Phil.

The children had been running after Thaddeus. They were gasping for breath.

"You kids!" cried Ranger Martin, astonished at the sight of them. "Come with us! Your lives are in danger!"

A tide of newborn Fabrinels—humanesque and bear—flowed over the rise behind the kids, and the rangers went pale.

One of the bears snapped its jaws—teeth gleaming like white daggers in a red pit, One of the humanesque's eyes pulsed fluorescent yellow, then violet.

Martin's legs wobbled like Jello, and Abigail let out a

low, panicked moan.

"It's okay," said Warren. "They're machines. Good machines."

"RUN!" Thaddeus cried, and the bewildered rangers sprinted away, tripping and stumbling as they fled.

Warren watched them flee, and when he turned back around, Mirra was there, gazing at him silently. He stared back and could feel Thaddeus, his friends and the assembled Fabrinels observing them.

"My son," Mirra whispered. She shook, and huge tears welled in her eyes. "I know you. I ..." Words failed her, but Warren embraced her warmly.

"I'm sorry," she said, "I'm so sorry."

Warren wanted to reassure her, but Thaddeus was clicking and snapping, and the hatchlings were suddenly in motion all around them.

"It's okay," Warren said. "I understand."

They turned together and saw Uhlgoth's Eltura charging uphill, weapons flashing in the sun. They were perhaps five hundred yards away now, and twenty or so hatchlings were rushing haphazardly down to meet them, firing arrows, throwing spears, and hurling rocks as they charged.

Compared to the Eltura's precise wedge, Thaddeus's troops looked like a disorganized rabble.

"They're coming for you, Goddess," Thaddeus said to Mirra. The mischievous twinkle was gone from the big man's eyes, and his warm, easygoing smile had been replaced by a look of profound concern.

Thaddeus's troops were attacking the enemy with a blizzard of projectiles, but none seemed to find a mark.

Explosions rocked the meadow, but nothing slowed the Eltura's relentless advance.

"There's something around them," whispered Phil, and Warren saw what she meant.

There was a sheen—a sort of clear, arching membrane—enveloping the entire unit. From certain angles, the membrane wasn't visible, but now and again it would glint and wobble, distorting the view of the soldiers inside.

The Eltura were running inside a kind of bubble—a vast translucent shield that enveloped them, moved with them. One of the Eltura—only one—wore a backpack. A glowing, basketball-sized orb was mounted on top of the pack. Warren wondered if it was responsible for the shield.

"They will have to turn the shield off to take you," Thaddeus said to Mirra.

"So what's our plan?" asked Sean. He sounded terrified.

The Eltura shield winked off suddenly and the soldiers within unleashed a volley of spears and arrows at Thaddeus's advance troops.

There were three blinding flashes in quick succession, and two of the hatchlings fell shrieking to the ground. Thaddeus's troops returned fire. Too late. The enemy's invincible shield had snapped back on.

Thaddeus issued a deafening chorus of new commands to his soldiers, then answered Sean's question.

"I will try to protect Mirra," he said. "But these are not ordinary Fabrinels."

He looked at Mirra. "They've been bred for one purpose, Goddess: to capture you and hold you until Uhlgoth arrives. They will slaughter anyone who tries to stop them."

Phil said, "So what are we supposed to do?"

"Hide," said Thaddeus. "Now. And for mercy's sake, stay out of sight until the fight is over."

Phil and Sean retreated uphill, but Warren stood his ground. "I'm staying," he said. "Go! It'll be okay. Hurry!"

Warren's friends turned and sprinted toward the crest of the ridge, and Warren turned to face the enemy once more. What he saw filled him with dread.

Twenty-four

The methodically advancing "V" was less than a hundred yards below them now and the size of the fighters was suddenly, alarmingly clear.

They looked to Warren like giants—each soldier a good foot taller than Thaddeus.

Warren glanced at his mother. Her tears had dried and she looked tired. Drained. What she was feeling as she watched the advancing line, he could not tell.

"Achak will come," Warren whispered. "And Ina. They'll help you fight, Thaddeus."

"Achak is dead," said Thaddeus, without taking his eyes off the Eltura. The words hit Warren like a fist.

"Dead? How?"

The Eltura were adjusting weapons now, preparing for the attack, and Warren could see their eyes: bright lanterns of yellow.

The captain, the creature at the center of the "V", stared at Warren. Their eyes met.

Four of Thaddeus's great bears hurled themselves at the shield surrounding the Eltura, roaring and bellowing. Some of the humanesques pummeled the shield walls with sofa-sized rocks ripped from the ground. Others leapt on top of the membrane and hacked at the shimmering envelope with knives and tomahawks.

From a distance, it looked like they were floating, hacking at the air itself.

The attack seemed to have no effect. The Eltura came confidently on.

"Achak is dead," said Thaddeus flatly, as he stepped toward the enemy, "but you could help me fight."

Warren glanced around, wondering what he meant. Sean and Phil had vanished.

"He means me," said Mirra, and Warren saw her shut her eyes.

Uhlgoth's soldiers were close now, and Warren wanted to run. The tips of their weapons glowed, and their faces were hard and cruel. Thaddeus clicked and bellowed, and the hatchlings suddenly fell back. Warren expected them to instantly regroup, to charge the oncoming force field again from all sides. But they did not. Instead, the humanesques fell to one knee and the bears dropped to all fours, to the sides of the shield wall.

"No! Don't give up!" Warren screamed. "Attack!"

But the force was no longer under his command and Thaddeus made no reply and never took his eyes off the enemy.

All at once, Warren understood. The undercharged hatchlings were wearing down. Thaddeus had stopped the futile assault to preserve what fight they had left.

Uhlgoth's force was fifty feet away, and now it was just Thaddeus, standing like a statue between the enemy and Warren and his mother.

Mirra stood erect also, face serene, eyes fixed on Uhlgoth's minions.

Warren touched her hand. Merely touched it. A simple gesture to let her know he was there.

A simple gesture.

But the slight contact nearly ripped him in half. To Warren it felt as if the meadow—*the entire ridge*—flipped. Rolled over on itself in a single gasp. Great spasms of energy coursed through his veins; pulled on him like G-forces.

It felt to the boy as if he'd fallen into a raging river. Dropped into a roaring avalanche.

His first impulse was to jump away, to leap back and break contact with his mother's hand. But he resisted. Steadied himself.

He knew this power. *Gaia's* power. He'd felt it before, at Pipestone Canyon, when—in his fury at Todd Jr.—he'd conjured the twister. He'd felt it at other times, too. Milder versions of it. Pulses of Earth energy, that he could not define or explain.

This was the same sensation, on steroids. *Times a thousand.* This was raw, planetary energy—the wild ferocity of the Living Earth flowing into one human: Mirra. Onatah. Chomolungma. Gaia. *His mother.*

Warren saw the Eltura shift suddenly inside their translucent bubble. The "V" dissolved. Soldiers changed positions, readying the capture.

A hurrying cloud blocked the sun, the sky grew dark,

and a fierce gust of wind blasted the ridge.

"Onatah!" Thaddeus cried, his long hair flying in the sudden gale. "Yes! Use your strength. DESTROY THEM!"

Warren held his mother's hand, and now he could feel her vast power coalescing, focusing; like millions of volts of electricity funneling into a single laser beam. She would blast the Eltura into oblivion.

But something was wrong.

Warren sensed it. Something was holding Mirra back. The Eltura were almost on top of them now but something was preventing her from pulling the trigger.

Fear.

The boy felt it as clearly as he felt the bright river of energy.

Mirra was afraid. She'd failed the last time she'd confronted Uhlgoth, and Eric Wilkes—Warren's father—was dead. What if she failed now? What if she couldn't protect her son?

Doubt blocked her destructive might like a dam on a raging river.

"You can do it!" Warren screamed. "You can!"

Mirra's face was a picture of torment.

"Do it!" Warren cried. "I believe in you!"

Mirra stared at the boy and her expression softened.

She smiled at her son. Her only son. Doubt and fear vanished. She knew what she had to do.

But now the enemy was leaping forward, rushing at them.

The translucent shield divided like an amoeba—with three Eltura in one half and four in the other.

Lightning blasted the cell on the left; the bolt so close

that Warren's skin prickled and he was momentarily blinded.

The shield wavered but held. And now the blob to Warren's right slammed into Thaddeus and rebounded, blowing the mountain man off his feet and back fifty yards.

In an instant the two halves were rushing back together, surrounding Warren and Mirra, trapping them in the middle, as Mirra's lightning pummeled the shields.

BOOM! Both shields failed and a fantastically powerful bolt vaporized two of the Eltura in their boots.

But the raid wasn't over.

Twenty-five

Savage hands ripped Warren from his mother's side and a bright blade flashed toward his throat.

"STOP!" boomed the Eltura captain, as Mirra lifted her hands toward the heavens. "Or the boy dies!"

Instantly, the lightning ceased. Mirra's arms fell to her sides.

"No!" Warren screamed. "Kill them!"

But the momentary pause was all the Eltura needed. Four of the hulking beasts seized Mirra and leapt downhill with her.

Warren caught a glint of metal as a syringe pierced his mother's neck.

"Mom!" he screamed. The Eltura captain sheathed his knife, tucked Warren under one vice-like arm, and leapt downhill.

Warren and his captor crashed and smashed their way

down slope like a runaway train. Warren saw the beast's free hand rising toward his face, one finger extended.

Except ... it wasn't a finger. It was a needle. The needle was part of the Fabrinel's hand. The creature was going to drug him. Warren jerked and twisted and pulled and kicked, fighting like a trapped animal. Fighting for his life.

He could not break loose—the Eltura's strength was that of a hundred men—but the boy's gyrations *did* force the creature to halt its careening descent to apply the syringe.

The monster paused on an outcropping of rock—small stones clattering around its feet—and brought the needle carefully to Warren's neck as its other hand held him motionless in mid air. The beast's yellow eyes glowed.

SMACK! A blunt blade smashed the monster's forearm just as the needle touched Warren's skin. The Eltura howled; so loud Warren thought his head would explode. And instantly the creature cast him aside. Warren flailed through the air and crashed onto steep ground. He rolled in the dirt and twisted around in time to see Thaddeus and the giant fighting like mad bulls.

It was a short fight.

Thaddeus's hatchlings arrived and swarmed the monster, piercing its thick hide with a dozen glowing spears. Warren leapt out of the way as the hulking beast crashed to earth, melting and disintegrating as it fell.

"Thaddeus!" Warren cried. The boy was scratched and bruised and bleeding, but to his own injuries he paid no heed. "They drugged her again!" he screamed. "She can't fight."

"Steady, lad." Thaddeus was staring at the knot of Eltura fleeing downhill, three hundred yards below them. Half of the hatchlings were in pursuit.

Thaddeus swung his tomahawk into his belt and crouched to leap downhill, when they both saw a miraculous sight.

Ina and twenty hatchlings were sweeping over a lip in the slope, directly in front of the fleeing Eltura. Warren shouted with joy. But then his glee turned to bewilderment.

SNAP! The Eltura's translucent shield flashed on once more and the bubble steamrolled Ina's force, tossing shrieking hatchlings in every direction.

The bubble then split into identical halves. And the halves instantly diverged.

One bubble continued downhill. The other veered sharply to the right, traveling laterally across the slope.

To Warren's eyes it looked as if the beings inside the two bubbles were the same. In fact, he could see his mother inside *both* bubbles.

Ina and the hatchlings hesitated. Then stormed after the bubble on the right.

"WAIT!" Thaddeus screamed, leaping forward.

Green lasers fired from both of the mountain man's eyes. Warren saw the beams hit the divergent bubbles.

"What's happening?" Warren cried.

"STOP!" Thaddeus screamed. "YOU'VE GOT THE WRONG ONE!"

Ina's force swarmed the right-hand bubble. They were around it. On top of it. Stabbing the translucent shell with spears and knives.

"GET AWAY!" thundered Thaddeus, "FALL BACK!"

Ina heard the big man's cries, but her fighters did not.

The fake shield exploded with a blinding white flash and a searing shock wave knocked Warren flat. The rumble and boom of the blast reverberated through the valley, ricocheting off granite cliffs and distant peaks.

The boy rolled, gasping, onto his knees in time to see the real Eltura guard—and the real Mirra—disappear into the forest at the bottom of the slope.

Mirra was Uhlgoth's prisoner now. Achak was dead. And half the hatchling army had been obliterated.

Twenty-six

The Eltura halted in a little glade, a few hundred yards inside the forest. Boulders littered the earth in all directions, and moss covered everything: the ground, the rocks, fallen trees and limbs. It was a quiet, cool place, even in the height of summer.

"We wait," said the Eltura captain. "Master will be here soon."

The soldiers carrying Mirra dumped her unceremoniously onto the ground, formed a circle around her body and turned out, weapons ready. Mirra lay limply on her back—eyes open and staring, face slack like a coma patient. Beads of sweat coated her skin and her breathing was shallow and rapid.

A cloaked form emerged like a phantom from an even darker part of the forest and approached the sentinels. They did not challenge the intruder, but allowed it inside their protective ring. The stranger knelt beside Mirra and threw back its hood.

It was the fake Mirra, eyes bright and curious. The fake pressed its hand against Mirra's forehead and held it there.

"Oh, so much fear," it cooed. "So much confusion and doubt and worry." The creature clasped Mirra's lifeless hand in a gesture of false compassion.

The ground shook suddenly, hard enough to send loose stones clattering off larger boulders. The fake Mirra smiled cruelly.

"You *should* be worried, Goddess. Already the master has entered your mind. Already he usurps your power. That was him just now. Can you not feel your power flowing into my lord?"

Slowly the fake lifted her fingertips from Mirra's forehead. "And now I've taken images of all of your companions," she said. "I know what they look like. I know where they are."

The fake stood and cast off her cloak. She was dressed exactly like Mirra. She removed the small dagger case from inside her jacket and opened it. The tip of the dagger still glowed brightly. She closed the case, gave Mirra one last, long look, turned and moved through the trees in the direction of the meadow. It was getting dark.

Twenty-seven

On the open ridge high above, Warren and Thaddeus stood together as Ina and fifteen hatchlings—all that remained—hurried toward them. Sean and Phil jogged in from the opposite direction.

"Warren!" cried Phil. "The light. The sky—what does it mean?"

Warren was wondering the same thing.

Daylight had been fading for the past fifteen minutes. The sun was setting.

Setting. At 4:30 in the afternoon, on a June day.

It was an impossible thing.

The group came together on the ridge and long shadows stabbed out over the meadow.

"Sunset's at, like, nine o'clock this time of year," panted Sean. "Isn't it?"

"Yeah," said Warren, who was still consumed with

thoughts of the battle and his mother's capture. "Around then."

They all stared as the sun touched the jagged, snow-mantled peaks to the west.

"Warren," said Phil. "Where's your mom? Could she … I mean … could she be causing this?"

Thaddeus answered. "It's Onatah's power," he said grimly. "But not Onatah's will."

Sean squinted at him. "What does that mean?"

"I don't understand," said Phil.

"Onatah was captured," said Ina patiently. "Now Uhlgoth is claiming her power."

"How?" said Warren, clawing his way out of his mental fog. "They just got her. Uhlgoth wasn't even there."

"It doesn't matter," said Thaddeus, and there was compassion in his ancient eyes. "Think back, lad, to your own encounter with Uhlgoth in the Chamber of the Stars. How he probed your mind. Spoke to you from afar."

Warren shuddered.

"Think back to how he seized Mr. Finley, took him over and broke his will."

Sean stammered, "But this? Making it dark four hours early? How? Why?"

The flaming orange sun vanished behind the distant peaks as the boy spoke.

"He's using Gaia's power to accelerate the Earth's rotation," said Thaddeus. "As to why …" The big man considered the question. "His ship is nearly here. Two hours away at most. It will touch down on this ridge and he wants cover." He looked at the fifteen surviving hatchlings sitting motionless, staring hard at the spot where the sun had just set, as if they might somehow will it to rise again. They had not had time to fully charge. "And he wants us weak."

"There's another reason," said Ina bitterly. "He's usurping her power because he can."

Tears welled in Warren's eyes and Phil clutched his hand.

"Uhlgoth has dreamed of enslaving Gaia for five centuries," Ina continued. "His dream is beginning to come true."

"*Beginning?*" Sean muttered.

"He's seizing Gaia's power," said Thaddeus, "but he doesn't understand the power yet. Gaia has secrets. Ancient knowledge beyond anything Uhlgoth has imagined. It will take time to tease the secrets out. It will take time to break her."

Warren stared at the horizon, and felt a new emotion rising inside him: rage.

"We have to get her back," he said thickly. "We will get her back."

Twenty-eight

Todd Jr. sat clutching the medallion in a small clearing one mile below the ridge. Uhlgoth's soldiers rested on the ground all around him. Junior guessed their number at about two thousand, though if his eyes had been shut, he might have guessed zero. There was no talking. Junior noticed with alarm that there was no breathing, either. There was no movement of any kind, in fact. Uhlgoth had shut his troops down with a burst of deafening clicks, and shut down they remained. It was an army of statues. And it gave Junior the creeps.

He stared, as a mosquito crawled across the face of the nearest soldier. The Fabrinel's eyes were open. The mosquito hopped onto the creature's gaping left eyeball and turned this way and that, seeking a blood vessel, but not finding one. The soldier did not blink.

Junior shivered. He knew the "statue soldiers" could

wake up in an instant. A command from his father was all it would take.

He turned three hundred and sixty degrees. Where *was* his father? The big man had hurried away with a small contingent of Fabrinels ten minutes earlier. Where had they gone? When would they return? Junior sat back and studied the medallion, which was still in its thick envelope of glass; or what looked like glass.

Truth be told, Junior felt better than he had in days. He'd found a US Army backpack at the edge of the clearing, and the pack was full of food: trail mix, Gatorade, Meals-Ready-to-Eat. Junior knew from TV that Meals-Ready-to-Eat, or MREs, were meals soldiers took into the field. It was bland, boring food. But it was food. And it was making him strong again.

Junior didn't want to think about the owner of the backpack, though he knew deep down that his father's troops had probably killed the person. The notion disturbed him greatly, so he tried to focus on the medallion. He'd asked his father if he could hold it. To his surprise, the big man had given it to him.

Junior gasped. The glass around the medallion was suddenly shrinking, melting; like ice. He cried out and dropped the relic on the ground.

"It's not my fault," he whispered, though no one was listening. "I didn't do anything!"

Junior glanced at the soldiers around him. No reaction. No movement. Not the faintest rustle.

Slowly, he retrieved the medallion. The glass envelope had vanished entirely and the gold felt heavy and smooth in his hand. He lifted the flashing relic to his eyes, and jammed his thumb against its obsidian core, thinking back to words his father had spoken hours earlier.

Professor Steele and Alvin Peeples (or rather, the disembodied machine intelligence of the two men) would "solve the riddle" of the medallion, his father had said. That was the reason for the glass envelope, Junior recalled. Bizarre as it seemed, Steele and Peeples had been circulating inside the glass, unlocking the relic's secrets.

Had they succeeded? Is that why the envelope was gone? Junior pressed the obsidian harder and suddenly something leapt from the relic into his head.

Two years earlier, Junior had been hit between the eyes with a fastball. This felt worse.

He dropped the medallion, clutched his scalp and rolled on the ground in agony. He twisted and writhed, tore at his hair and cried out. But the bright starburst of pain receded as quickly as it had started. Ten seconds more and Junior was in a kneeling position, gasping and probing his forehead, feeling for the wound. A projectile had blasted through his skull, or so it felt. But there was no mark. No blood. No pain.

There was, however, knowledge.

"The treasure ..." he whispered, falling back into a seated position as fresh insight unfurled like a vast, colorful mural in his mind.

His father had told him that the medallion held the secret to a spectacular treasure; a treasure the Mendari had intended to give the Denelai Indians when they departed Earth five hundred years earlier. His father was correct. *Sort of.*

Junior shut his eyes and let the new knowledge continue to unfold in his mind.

The treasure was indeed spectacular. Fabulous beyond

imagination. But it wasn't what his father was expecting. It wasn't gold or diamonds or emeralds. The gift the Mendari lords had intended to give the Denelai all those centuries ago was worth more than a mountain of gold, Junior could see that clearly now.

He shivered. His father would do great evil with this gift once he learned of it.

Twenty-nine

Junior heard voices. Uhlgoth and his small contingent of soldiers were returning.

The boy thrust the heavy medallion deep into his jacket pocket where it hung like a stone. Maybe Uhlgoth would forget about the medallion. Junior doubted it, but decided to keep the relic hidden for the time being.

The statue army, still frozen, looked creepier than ever in the gathering gloom.

Junior looked around.

Wasn't it awfully early to be getting dark? And wasn't the light fading unusually fast? It seemed so to the boy, though he couldn't be sure. The truth was, Junior spent so much time indoors, playing video games and watching TV, that he had little sense for the natural world. The growing darkness disturbed him nonetheless, and only heightened his sense of dread.

Uhlgoth and his men burst suddenly from the trees, dragging three large, sticky-wet bundles.

Todd Jr. watched them wind their way through the statue army and realized with horror that the bundles weren't bundles, but men. US Army soldiers. And the sticky, oozy stuff that shone in the dying light was blood. The soldiers were covered in blood.

Uhlgoth's Fabrinels released the prisoners a few feet from Todd Jr. and jerked them into standing positions. The men were alive, barely. One teetered and fell, only to be yanked upright once more.

"Captain Bentz," said Uhlgoth, stepping in front of the middle soldier. The man's head hung like a weight and his scalp was so gashed and bloody Todd Jr. could barely look at it.

The two other men appeared equally battered. Uhlgoth thrust something in front of Bentz's eyes. "This is your satellite phone. You will call your commander. The one in charge of this campaign. So that I may speak with him."

Bentz lifted his head slowly and stared at Uhlgoth as Junior gawked. Bentz's face was filthy and bleeding, but his eyes were clear. Bright. Defiant.

"Go to hell," he rasped.

Uhlgoth twitched ever so slightly and one of his minions seized the soldier to Bentz's right, by the throat.

Todd Jr. buried his head in his hands as the Fabrinel crushed the soldier's windpipe with one iron hand. The man's gurgling, gasping death noises bore into Junior's brain, too horrible to bear.

"You will call your commander," said Uhlgoth. "Now."

Thirty

It was fully dark when Warren and company crept within three hundred yards of the Eltura soldiers holding Mirra prisoner.

Stars blazed overhead and the broad band of the Milky Way resembled a great, placid river across the heavens. It was a surreal, inconceivable panorama for half past five on a summer afternoon. It was getting colder, too. Warren guessed the temperature had dropped fifteen degrees in the preceding hour.

Thaddeus whispered for the group to halt, and the entire crowd—the three children, Ina, and the fifteen surviving hatchings—sat quietly in a circle around him.

They were still in open meadow, but tree line was a stone's throw below them now, and they could clearly see the forest edge: a dark, looming wall against an ocean of bright stars.

The forest itself wasn't completely dark. There was a faint blue glow beneath the canopy directly down slope.

Phil noticed it first and nudged Warren. "Is that … is that where they have your mom, Warren?"

Thaddeus answered from the darkness near at hand. "Yes. Onatah is there, guarded all around by Eltura."

"And Uhlgoth?" said Warren.

Thaddeus leaned closer to the boy. "Not here yet. Eltura only, waiting for their master to arrive." He hesitated, then said. "Lad, if we're to attempt a rescue, it must be now."

Warren nodded, eyes wide in the dark. Phil and Sean strained to hear the big man's words.

"Mirra is held at present by four fighters only. Fearsome strong they are, true. But once Uhlgoth arrives with the rest of his lot …"

"I understand," said Warren. "I'm ready."

The big man looked side to side and whispered.

"Can you feel your mother's strength, lad?"

Warren thought about it.

"I can feel it," he said at last. "When we're walking out here," he gestured to the wilderness around them. "There are places on the ground, certain places, here and there, where I feel it. Like electricity, sort of."

"Power wells," whispered Ina. "You're talking about power wells."

Warren had no idea what she meant.

"Lad," Thaddeus continued, "can you use the power you're feeling? Can you harness it?"

"No," said Warren. "I mean, I don't know." He stammered, "I … it's not like that. Not like when *she* uses it. It's not mine."

"But I've seen you do it!" whispered Sean. "The tornado … after Todd Jr. stole the medallion. Remember?"

"You made a tornado?" said Phil, from the blackness on Warren's left.

"Yes, but I wasn't trying to do that," said Warren. "It just happened. I stepped on one of those whatchamacallits …"

"Power wells," said Thaddeus. "Fonts of Earth energy they are."

"Yes, but it was an accident. I didn't try to conjure a tornado. It just happened."

"Lad," said the mountain man. "We need you to try now." He glanced at Ina. "Ina and myself, and the hatchlings here … we'll rush the enemy. Fight like mad dogs we will, to save Onatah. You know that. But if the Eltura put their shield on again, we'll be at a loss. We need your help. *I* need your help."

It felt to Warren like the entire group was staring at him, though he couldn't see their faces in the dark.

"I understand," he said. "I'll try."

Thaddeus leaned back. "Good lad."

A sliver of moon stabbed over the peaks to the east and bathed the meadow in a sudden, silvery glow. Warren turned and saw the ghostly outline of the fire lookout, standing sentinel-like on the ridge top half a mile away.

"Let's move," hissed the mountain man. He started to rise, then froze. Ina went rigid, too, and Warren saw her hand curl around her spear. He followed her gaze and saw what she was looking at.

Someone was climbing up the slope toward them.

The humanesque hatchlings raised their weapons. The bears growled softly, revealing rows of white, dagger teeth.

"Hold," murmured Thaddeus to the group, as the figure drew closer.

The stranger called out softly. "Warren?" It was a female voice, soothing and familiar. "Warren? Where are you?"

The words seemed to float on the cool, moonlit air, and Warren felt a surge of nearly unbearable joy well up inside him.

Thaddeus gripped his shoulder. "Hold," he whispered.

The stranger ascended a sharp step in the meadow, drew level with the group, and came forward.

"Warren," she called again, in her soft, plaintive voice. "Are you here?"

The woman turned as she wound her way closer, and the group beheld her profile against the rising moon.

It was Mirra.

Thirty-one

Uhlgoth spoke into Captain Bentz's satellite phone as Todd Jr. listened.

"General Edwards," said Uhlgoth, with false concern. "You've lost many fine men today. Too many brave soldiers like Captain Bentz here."

Bentz teetered like a drunk. A Fabrinel heaved him into a standing position once more and jerked his head back. Bentz's eyes were swollen so severely, Todd Jr. couldn't tell if they were open or shut.

"Who are you?" General Edwards demanded. "And what do you want?"

Todd Jr. could hear the gruff, middle-aged voice on the other end of the call and tried to picture the man, standing in a war room someplace; one among hundreds of military and law enforcement personnel scrambling to figure out what was happening in the North Cascades.

"Police and FBI agents are dead also," Uhlgoth continued. "Civilians, too. And now a great, unexplained darkness has fallen over the land … and over the hearts of your people."

"What do you want?" repeated the general.

"I want you to leave this area unpatrolled and unmolested," said Uhlgoth, "until we depart one hour from now. Or tens of thousands more will die."

Edwards's reply was crisp and official. "We do not negotiate with terrorists. And we do not take kindly to threats."

Uhlgoth ignored him. "Some of your colleagues are discussing a nuclear strike, general. We know this. We are monitoring your communications."

If the general was surprised, he concealed it. "Listen to me, you son of a bitch," he said. "You have entered and occupied US territory illegally. You do not dictate terms. We do. Lay down your arms and surrender. Now."

"YOU WILL MAKE NO STRIKE!" Uhlgoth screamed. "If you initiate a strike, I will know. And the consequences will be severe."

"I repeat," said the general. "We do not negotiate with terrorists. Lay down your arms and surrender."

"General," said Uhlgoth, his tone morphing from pleasant to savage, "I do not require negotiation. I require obedience. Obey me."

"Go to hell," said Edwards, and Todd Jr. could hear him handing off his phone.

"General!" said Uhlgoth quickly. "Wait."

Edwards came on again. "Surrender," he said. "*Now.*"

"General," said Uhlgoth. "Thirty seconds from now, Los Angeles will suffer a magnitude eight earthquake. I will stay on the line as you confirm this."

Uhlgoth switched the phone to speaker mode and set it on a rock. Then he planted his feet, shut his eyes, and stood still. As still, it seemed to Junior, as the Fabrinel fighters sitting statue-like all around him.

Uhlgoth's eyes flashed open and a mile away, Mirra screamed in agony. Uhlgoth smiled. Part of him was inside her mind now, unlocking her secrets, usurping her power.

One minute passed. The phone was silent and Junior cocked his head. Had the call gone dead?

Two of Uhlgoth's Fabrinels projected bright holograms filled with rapidly changing maps and images. Uhlgoth stepped inside the flickering, wedge-shaped displays, studying them closely.

Ninety seconds. There was a sudden hum of voices on the other end of the satellite call. Terse commands, then shouting followed by bursts of heavy static. And suddenly the general was back on the line. He sounded shaken.

"How are you doing this?" he asked.

"All of Earth's living systems are now in my control, general," Uhlgoth proclaimed, clearly relishing his new-found might. "Wind and wave. Earth and sky. Molten rock and polar ice. The wild heart of your planet has been bludgeoned into submission. Mother Nature is my slave, general, which means you are my slave. Obey me or face annihilation."

Thirty-two

Warren couldn't believe his eyes. His mother was walking slowly toward them in the moonlight. Somehow, she had escaped the Eltura, and the only reason Warren wasn't rushing out to greet her was that Thaddeus was holding him back.

"Patience," breathed the big man, one great hand pressing down on Warren's shoulder as they crouched in the gloomy hollow. "Patience."

Ina and the other Fabrinels waited and watched; tense as mountain lions. Sean and Phil scarcely dared to breath.

"Patience."

"Warren?" came his mother's familiar voice. "Warren? Are you here? Please, Warren. I'm hurt. They hurt me."

To hell with patience. Warren twisted free of Thaddeus's grasp and bounded into the open.

"Here, Mom! I'm here! Just a little farther!"

Warren stumbled through the brush, but within two steps knew something was wrong. Mirra was running toward him, accelerating as she came, eyes flashing in the moonlight.

"Fake!" screamed Phil. "She's a fake, Warren, look out!"

Warren dove clear as the Fabrinel shot forward, quick as a leaping wolf. But she wasn't aiming for the boy. Her dagger was out, burning like a white-hot flare, and suddenly she was among the hatchlings.

Warren had never seen anything move so fast. In an eye blink she was in their midst, spinning and twisting, nicking every hatchling with her poison blade.

Thaddeus roared, smashed the fake in the face, and knocked her across the hill into the darkness. But the damage was done.

All around, hatchlings crashed and crumpled into the dirt, their cries echoing off the rocks.

And suddenly the fake was back, shooting out of the darkness like some underworld demon; molten-tipped blade lighting up the slope as it came, this time straight for the boy.

What happened next would remain forever seared in Warren's brain.

The fake streaked toward him, demon eyes flashing. Thaddeus stepped in its path, and the creature darted left. Suddenly, Ina exploded out of the darkness and rammed her spear into the monster's side. The fake stumbled and bellowed like a skewered buffalo. But before it fell, it heaved its poison blade—straight at Warren's face.

Molten steel flashed through the darkness. The blade was going to strike him. There was nothing he could do.

No way he could move aside fast enough.

Then Thaddeus raised his left hand and caught the weapon, point first.

"Thaddeus!" Warren screamed, as the tip sliced into the mountain man's hand. "No!"

Thaddeus was a Fabrinel. The blade was tipped with cyber toxin. In a couple of seconds, the big man would implode; would wither and desiccate like plastic in a fire.

"Thaddeus!"

The mountain man dropped to his knees and stretched his wounded arm on a rock. Other hand gripping his tomahawk, he reared back and swung down, smashing with all his might, severing his own hand in one terrible, stupendous blow.

"That's better," he said, getting to his feet once more.

Warren gaped as Sean and Phil emerged from hiding places. The moon had painted the entire ridge silver white.

"But, the toxin," gasped Warren. As he spoke, Thaddeus's severed hand shriveled and melted into the dirt at their feet.

"Caught it in time," said Thaddeus. His massive left forearm now ended in a clean, flat stump. There was no blood. Instead, the stump glowed faintly.

"But I wasn't fast enough to stop that devil," he said, gazing around at where the fake had slaughtered his fighters.

Here and there, the remains of the hatchlings continue to sizzle and hiss, as their once invincible bodies melted into nothingness. The fake Mirra had killed them all, and the big man roared as he absorbed the devastation. It was a shoulders-back, full-throated cry of rage and anguish, a thunderous bellow that shook the ground.

Ina just glared at the Eltura camp in the glade below and said nothing.

"It's my fault," said Warren miserably. "If I hadn't run out to her …"

"Lad," Thaddeus rumbled, composing himself and stooping to peer at the boy. "Don't. You thought it was your ma. Truth be told, the devil had me fooled."

"She sounded exactly like your mom," said Sean. "I thought it was her. I thought she'd escaped."

Warren felt like vomiting. It was almost more than he could absorb. In a few moments, Uhlgoth's fake had obliterated their tiny army. An army Thaddeus and Achak had nurtured and cajoled to life. The demon had also cost Thaddeus his hand. It was too much for the boy to take in.

"Guys!" whispered Sean. "Check it out." He was craning his neck and they all followed his gaze. "Helicopters."

Thirty-three

High overhead, an armada of red lights was descending slowly through the atmosphere. The bright moon illuminated fragments of metal here and there; bits of craft amid the light. But nothing was clearly defined.

"Lots of helicopters," Sean said hopefully. Then his voice wavered. "Only, there's no sound."

Thaddeus lowered his gaze and pyramid-shaped holograms burst from his right eye in nanosecond flashes. The eerie green images changed so fast the children couldn't grasp them. But Ina understood.

"They're not helicopters," she said, as Thaddeus's 3-D projections winked out. "It's a ship. Uhlgoth's ship."

Sean's gaze never left the slowly-descending lights. "But then, okay, our guys will see it, right?" He sounded desperate. "The Air Force will see it and shoot it down. They're probably getting ready to fire now. We better move."

"There will be no response," said Ina. "The military is staying away."

Sean started to protest, when Phil said, "Where's Warren?"

A heavy cloud drifted in front of the moon, and the meadow's silvery aura changed to blood red beneath the steadily descending ship.

"Warren Wilkes!" Phil cried. "Warren?"

The others called as well, but there was no reply. The boy was gone.

Thirty-four

Todd Jr. hustled along in the center of Uhlgoth's army as the swarm hurried through deep forest. All around him, Fabrinel soldiers crashed and smashed their way forward, plowing through thick brush and mowing down small trees. But there was no talking. No breathing either—aside from his own pained gasps.

Shafts of silvery moonlight stabbed through the canopy here and there, but not enough so Todd Jr. could see where he was going. Many times he stumbled and fell, banging his shins on unseen logs and whacking his head or cutting his hands on sharp thorns as he went down. He was bruised, breathing hard and sweating heavily when at last they entered the glade where Mirra was being held prisoner.

The trees here were immense. The glade was dark. But there was a faint, soft light enveloping the patch of earth where Mirra lay.

Todd Jr. stepped closer and forgot his bruises and burning lungs. The woman on the ground was beautiful, but so pale he thought at first she must be dead. Then he saw her chest rise and fall and felt a wave of relief. She wasn't dead. His father hadn't killed her. Not yet.

The light puzzled the boy ... the soft glow enveloping Mirra. He looked up.

It wasn't moonlight. The moon was low in the sky and the trees here were tall and thick. Moonlight couldn't penetrate.

Junior scratched his head. Was the light coming from the Eltura guards? He didn't think so.

He stepped closer to Mirra. There was nothing artificial about this light. Nothing mechanical or high-tech. Rather, the light was, was ...

The boy struggled for the word. It wasn't a word he'd heard very often. It wasn't a word he used. But it came to him anyway. *Holy.*

This light was holy. And seeing it now gave him the oddest feeling.

Uhlgoth clicked half a dozen times, the Eltura guards jerked Mirra's limp body out of the dirt, Junior snapped out of his reverie, and the hoard continued running, out of the forest and onto the steep, wide-open ridge.

Straight uphill they ran then. Todd Jr. gasped for breath and his heart boomed in his ears.

At Uhlgoth's command the swarm halted at last, after a long, brutal push, and Junior collapsed like a wounded animal in the grass.

When he finally lifted his head he saw that they'd reached the top of the ridge and were sitting at the edge of a wide, flat meadow. A fire lookout stood near the center of the meadow.

The deathly quiet of the place, and the lookout's dark, shuttered windows (the tower had been evacuated hours earlier) only heightened Junior's misery and feelings of loneliness.

The massive steel legs of the tower glinted in the moonlight. Junior stared and saw the glint change from silver to red. Red light reflected off the tower's antennas and solar panels, and now the same eerie red glow swallowed the meadow.

For a moment, Junior thought he was seeing the reflection of a forest fire. Then he looked up, and grasped what was really happening. A great ship was descending slowly through the atmosphere, coming down to land in the meadow. It was his father's ship. It was real. And the sight of it filled him with dread.

The Fabrinel army fell quickly into formation, and Uhlgoth prepared to address his troops.

The Eltura had thrown Mirra onto a low, flat rock. Her head was bleeding and her skin looked paler than ever. On hands and knees Junior crept toward her, then paused, sat back, and studied the Eltura guards. There were four guards arrayed evenly around Mirra's limp body. They were facing out, weapons ready.

Junior crawled between the two nearest sentries, wondering if they would stab him in the back and half hoping that they would.

But the guards moved not a millimeter. Apparently, they didn't consider the boy a threat.

Junior crawled on, and stopped a few inches from Mirra's face. "Are you alive?" he whispered.

No response.

He studied the cut on Mirra's forehead. It was a nasty gash, slowly oozing blood.

"Might need stitches for that," he said gently.

The holy aura that had transfixed the boy in the glade enveloped Mirra still, but the aura seemed to be fading, giving way to the blood-red glow from Uhlgoth's ship.

"Can you hear me?" Junior whispered. He waited, watching Mirra breath, then said, "I know your son."

Mirra did not stir, and Junior brushed tears from his eyes. The tears flowed.

Maybe it was because of all he'd been through the last two days. Maybe it was because he missed his own mother so much and believed deep down that he'd never see her again. Maybe he cried because of Mirra's fragile appearance, and because the holy light was dying even as he watched.

Junior glanced at the Eltura guards, then leaned closer to Mirra.

"I'm sorry," he said miserably. "I'm so sorry. If I hadn't stolen the medallion from Warren, we wouldn't be here now. My dad would still be my dad."

Tears rolled down the boy's cheeks. "All those soldiers and police," he whispered. "They'd still be alive."

Mirra lay impassive on the cold stone, giving no sign that she'd heard anything he'd said. Still, he felt better for speaking. Mirra's peaceful countenance, and the strange, holy aura, comforted the boy, and he was seized with the desire to comfort her back, to ease her suffering … if he could.

Gently, he brushed the hair from Mirra's forehead, careful to avoid her cut.

"If I had some water and a First Aid kit, I could clean that up," he whispered. He had neither. And anyway, time seemed to be running out. With a heavy sob, he took Mirra's hand and held it tight.

Thirty-five

Ina, Thaddeus, Sean and Phil sat amid a cluster of stunted, wind-bent trees, not far from Todd Jr.

The bright moon vanished behind sullen clouds, and red light from Uhlgoth's slowly descending ship illuminated his waiting army.

Phil scanned the meadow, but the red light revealed little of the larger landscape. In the evil half-light, clusters of boulders and small trees became ghoulish, misshapen beasts, and the fire lookout resembled a monstrous robot waiting to be switched on.

Phil shivered. "Where's Warren now?" she asked, for at least the third time since the group had moved uphill in advance of Uhlgoth's army.

"Still close at hand, lass," answered Thaddeus. "Still trying."

Phil knew what the big man meant. Warren was

somewhere nearby trying to find a "power well," whatever that was. As Sean had told her, Warren had used one days earlier to summon a tornado.

Ina turned to the children in the darkness and took their hands.

"Listen to me," she whispered. "Uhlgoth's entire force is here, on the ridge. Which means that at the moment there aren't any Fabrinels in the surrounding meadows or forests. This is your chance to flee, and I implore you to take it. Run. Run through the night. Get as far from here as you can."

"All of the valleys have trails," added Thaddeus. "Find one and stay on it. Head downhill. Help will find you." He peered at them in the gloom. "Go now. Before the ship touches down."

Even as Thaddeus spoke, Uhlgoth's ship appeared to pause in its descent. Phil guessed it was two thousand feet above the ridge.

"If Uhlgoth succeeds," Phil whispered, "if he takes Warren's mother onto his ship and leaves … what will happen?"

Thaddeus sighed. "He won't leave, is my view." He nodded at the ship high above. "This vessel was built with Onatah in mind. It's a prison and a laboratory. He doesn't need to take her anywhere. He'll most likely sit in low-earth orbit and work on her 'til she breaks. 'Til he knows all her secrets and unravels all her mysteries."

"Then what?" said Sean.

"The death of Gaia," answered Phil. "The death of nature."

"Not just nature, lass," whispered Thaddeus. "The death of beauty, also. The death of mystery and wonder.

The death of hope itself." He glanced at Uhlgoth's army and the children glimpsed the outline of his great, shaggy beard as he turned.

"'*In wilderness is the preservation of all things*,' a great man once said. And he spoke true."

"But what's going to happen?" cried Sean. "To us? To people? To Warren? What about ..."

Uhlgoth's voice boomed over the dark meadow, silencing Sean and the others.

The prison ship hung in the air above them, sullen and menacing; a twinkling beacon of coming disaster.

"My friends," Uhlgoth proclaimed to his troops. "Victory is at hand."

Thirty-six

On the ground, a few feet from Uhlgoth, Todd Jr. squeezed Mirra's hand and whispered in her ear. "Can you hear me?" he asked. "Please, you need to wake up."

Junior glanced at Uhlgoth. He was facing the other way, addressing his army.

"He means to hurt you," Junior hissed. "He'll do it, too. I've seen him do horrible things. You need to wake up."

Mirra made no reply and her serene countenance did not change. But it seemed to Junior that the holy aura was weaker than ever. It had almost disappeared.

"Please," Todd Jr. begged, and with his free hand he found the medallion in his pocket and placed his thumb on the relic's obsidian heart.

No pictures flashed in Junior's mind this time, no

bright images of "treasure," or forgotten places. Now there was only a voice. A lone, male voice chanting softly, rhythmically, in a Native American tongue. The voice was haunting, mysterious. Junior tried to focus on the chant, but Uhlgoth was booming like a megaphone.

"You are to be leaders—generals—in a much larger army," Uhlgoth declared to his troops. "In the coming days, as I hold in orbit, dissecting our prize, you will fan out across the land, bringing order and discipline to a savage and unclean world."

Todd Jr. shut his eyes and forced his father's raving from his mind. He needed to focus on the chant. There was something special and important about this chant. Though he couldn't understand a syllable of the ancient tongue, he knew in his bones that it was playing now for a reason, that he was meant to hear it.

In fact, the rhythmic, hypnotic words Todd Jr. absorbed now were the same words Warren had heard when he first touched the medallion. Warren never grasped the meaning of the soft, repeating phrases, but Junior was desperate to understand them.

The strange music coursed through him now; fanning out from his core, causing his toes and fingers to tingle and vibrate.

Somehow, the chant was growing in power and intensity.

Todd Jr. was still clutching Mirra's hand, and apparently she could feel the music, too. She stirred suddenly and her lips moved.

Junior leaned close, straining to hear. "What did you say?" he whispered. "Please! I couldn't hear you. Please help me understand."

"He will kill you," she breathed.

Junior glanced at his father, who was still busy addressing his minions.

"Tell me what I need to do," the boy said firmly. "I want to help."

Mirra struggled against the drugs the Eltura had given her. Her lips moved again, and this time she uttered a single syllable: "Sing," she whispered.

Todd Jr. thought she must be delirious.

Uhlgoth's voice boomed over the meadow as his ship rotated high above, glinting like a ruby.

"Thousands more fighters will awaken tomorrow," Uhlgoth cried. "And in the coming days."

"Sing?" said Junior. "What do you mean? Sing what?"

And then it came to him. Mirra wanted him to chant. To repeat the words he was hearing as he touched the medallion.

"Me?" he protested. "But I don't know the language. I don't know what the words mean. And anyway, I can't sing."

"Please." Mirra's eyes flashed open and huge tears welled up. "Sing. Set me free."

"Set you free?"

Todd Jr. heard a short, sharp *CLICK,* and looked up. To his horror, one of the Eltura guards had turned completely around and was now studying Mirra closely. The creature's right index finger was also a sort of syringe. It was filling with liquid.

Junior put his mouth next to Mirra's ear. "Go limp," he whispered. "Shut your eyes and don't talk again."

Mirra did as he said. Her head tumbled to one side and her jaw went slack.

The sentinel stared at her curiously, but the syringe stopped filling.

It's like it doesn't even see me, Junior thought. Indeed, the creature appeared to be looking right through him. After a moment, it turned back around.

Junior shut his eyes and pressed his thumb harder into the medallion's obsidian core.

Nearby, Uhlgoth appeared to be nearing the end of his speech, which was now a combination of words and loud clicks and pops.

"You will turn the savages' own weapons against them," he roared. "You will rid the planet of the human scourge …"

Todd Jr. forced his father's diatribe from his mind once more and concentrated on the music flowing from the medallion.

It wasn't easy.

The music was strange and complex. Full of subtle tones and nuance. There was no way he could accurately repeat it. No possible way. Still, he had to try.

Leaning close to Mirra's ear, he shut his eyes and began.

"Ha-teesh wa, me-sa, ha-teesh nay, koh wa."

Junior gasped. The voice was his own, but the *words* were coming from another place. More miraculous still, the words were taking shape in his brain.

"Lay-ka-tee, oh ma, lay ma ha, teesh hoh," he cooed.

As Todd Jr. sang—whispering low and soft in Mirra's ear—he began to see pictures in his mind, of places and people long vanished. And all at once, like an unfamiliar object that suddenly becomes recognizable upon closer inspection, the meaning of the song crystallized in his mind. His heart thudded.

"Meh oh wah, meh oh way ..."

Bits of his father's raving seeped into his consciousness as he chanted.

"Remake the planet ... bringing progress and order ... secrets unlocked ... Earth ... as a model for enslaving other living planets across the galaxy ..."

Junior focused hard.

"Keh-oh-ley, ma chey koh va. Oh vay, oh tah ..."

" ... Stab the Wild Spirit in the heart, so that it can never re-grow, never again infect the minds of ..."

Uhlgoth stopped mid-sentence and Junior's blood froze. He knew without a doubt that his father had suddenly become aware of what he was doing.

"STOP!" Uhlgoth thundered, and Junior heard the El-tura—and the entire army behind them—turn in his direction.

But the boy did not look up. He had to finish the song. There could be no break.

"Mey te wa, oh key way, oh may na-cha-po, oh-vay sa," he sang. Slowly. Evenly.

There were three verses left to sing. He could see the verses coming at him in his mind now, forming precisely before he voiced them.

"KILL HIM!" Uhlgoth screamed.

Junior could not rush the lines, or slur or abbreviate them. The song would fail if he did that. The song required an exact pace and meter.

The boy suppressed his terror, mastered the adrenaline surging through his veins and ignored the impulses screaming at him to run. Yet he knew in his bones that he would never finish the song. There wasn't time. Any moment now he would be impaled by spear or arrow or knife. Any moment.

CRACK! BOOM! A spectacular flash of lightning lit up the ridge, turning night into day and momentarily freezing Uhlgoth's troops in their tracks.

CRASH! BOOM! A vast, flaming metal plate plunged knife-like into the meadow in the midst of Uhlgoth's army, crushing and impaling six of Uhlgoth's Fabrinels as it stabbed the earth.

Junior kept chanting.

The lightning bolt had hit Uhlgoth's ship.

"IT'S THE EARTH WITCH'S SON!" Uhlgoth shrieked. "FIND HIM!"

"Un teesh lay, ney sa ka, va teesh oh may, ka-po sa dey ... "

Todd Jr. breathed the last syllable of the chant into Mirra's ear just as his father ripped him off the ground and lifted him high into the air.

"Where is she?" the big man screamed; mouth foaming, face twisted with insane rage.

The song had worked. Somehow, the words had done their magic.

Junior had set Mirra free.

"WHERE IS SHE?"

Junior looked down at Mirra and saw her exhale for the last time. Her body went limp.

Uhlgoth howled and threw his son a hundred feet down slope. Then he turned, ripped a spear from one of the Eltura Guards, and stabbed the creature in the heart.

"No!" Uhlgoth shrieked. "No!"

There was another blinding flash and Uhlgoth's blood-red ship began to descend.

Thirty-seven

A knot of Uhlgoth's soldiers rushed out of the darkness, clutching Warren Wilkes in iron hands.

Fierce and wild Warren looked. Defiant and unafraid. It was not hard to imagine that he had summoned the lightning.

Uhlgoth grabbed a fistful of the boy's hair, jerked his head back, and with his other hand lifted a razor-edged knife to Warren's throat.

"Surrender to me!" Uhlgoth screamed. "Or the boy dies!"

Warren shut his eyes and felt his mother's power surging through the meadows all around him. He'd felt her presence more and more clearly over the past few minutes. He didn't know about the chant or what Todd Jr. had done. But wandering in the darkness, he'd felt her power building. Indeed, the entire ridge seemed to have become a power well.

"Surrender now!" Uhlgoth screamed, pressing the knifepoint so that it broke Warren's skin.

Warren focused on his hatred for Uhlgoth and summoned another stupendous lightning bolt. In the blinding flash he saw Uhlgoth's leering hoard massed on the meadow all around. He saw Uhlgoth, huge and terrifying, facial muscles drawn tight with rabid fury. And he saw his mother's body, limp and lifeless on the flat rock nearby. She looked dead. And yet … he could feel her energy humming and crackling through the ground beneath his feet.

"Where are you?" the boy whispered, struggling to comprehend. "What's happening?"

BOOM! FLASH! Warren called forth another burst of lightning without meaning to. Gaia's power was a clumsy, blunt instrument in his hands. A sledgehammer wielded by a blind man. He could not control his actions.

Uhlgoth clicked like an insect and one of the Eltura sentinels clasped Warren's right forearm between wrist and elbow and twisted the appendage like a dishrag, breaking Warren's bones with a loud *SNAP! SNAP!*

Warren howled in agony and saw bright explosions in his head.

"SURRENDER!" Uhlgoth shrieked at the darkness.

The sentinel twisted Warren's arm further, and the boy swooned and blacked out. The pain was too much. He would have fallen, but Uhlgoth held him upright by his hair.

Uhlgoth's ship came lower, red and pulsing, like a dying sun about to supernova.

And now Uhlgoth's voice was choked and mangled.

"Onatah!" he cried, driving the knifepoint deeper into Warren's neck. "Surrender to me!"

WHUMP! Warren heard the strange, sudden sound and looked up into the cruel, iridescent eyes of the Blank Frame crushing his arm. The Sentinel's eyes bulged suddenly; so severely Warren thought they might explode.

The beast released his arm and began convulsing, clawing frantically at something behind it. Its knees buckled and Warren and Uhlgoth saw that the "something" was a thick, glowing spear. The warrior that had delivered the weapon was there, too. It was Ina.

WHUMP! CRACK! A second spear whistled down, out of the darkness from the opposite side, knocking the knife from Uhlgoth's hand.

Warren caught the briefest glimpse then of a great, bearded freight train of a man exploding out of the darkness. With a roar, the bearded giant flattened Uhlgoth and Warren together; severing Uhlgoth's hold on the boy's hair. Warren landed hard on his tortured arm, and vomited the air from his lungs.

"MOVE!" Ina screamed, and Warren twisted in the dirt, bright ribbons of pain lighting up the inside of his skull as brilliantly as the bolts pummeling the meadow. Frantically, he kicked the ground, scrambling to back up, to keep from being trampled.

Ina and Thaddeus had come to his rescue. But looking up, Warren felt only dread. No way could they win this fight. Uhlgoth's soldiers were swarming in from all sides. A hundred spear and arrow points were rising in unison.

Uhlgoth was on his feet again. "Kill them all!" he screamed.

There was no escape.

But Ina and Thaddeus weren't trying to escape.

Quick as a rattlesnake, Ina dove for the legs of the El-tura fighter carrying the shield generator. As the creature fell, Thaddeus stabbed it in the side, ripped the glowing orb from its back and triggered the device, one handed, using his stump arm to hold the orb motionless. It all happened in an eye blink.

SNAP! A shimmering veil enveloped Warren, Mirra's inert body, Ina and Thaddeus as a hundred glowing spears and arrows pummeled the shield, exploding like fireworks.

Thaddeus manipulated the orb and a bright finger of the translucent shield material shot into the darkness, blowing Fabrinel soldiers out of the way as it expanded, seventy, eighty feet.

The bright corridor retracted quickly, pulling two tumbling, screaming shapes with it. Warren stared as Sean and Phil came to rest before him.

The children blinked at each other and Warren sat up, cradling his mangled arm. One of the bones was jutting through the skin, jagged and sharp like broken glass. He felt dizzy and sick to his stomach.

Thaddeus and Ina knelt next to Mirra's body as a blizzard of spears and arrows battered the pulsing, vibrating shield wall.

They could hear Uhlgoth's muffled screaming outside, and see shapes swirling in the blackness just beyond the membrane.

An Eltura sentinel rolled silently out of the grass at the edge of the dome and uncoiled like a viper. For a split second, Warren—his brain fogged by pain—thought the beast was outside the translucent wall.

It wasn't.

It had been hiding in the dark at the edge of the dome and now was rearing back, about to plunge a spear into Thaddeus's spine.

"Thaddeus!" Warren screamed. "Look out!"

The big man turned and Warren caught a flash of movement, a shape speeding in from the other direction.

It was Phil, diving toward the sentinel like an outfielder leaping for a ball. In her right hand she held a gleaming dagger.

The blade nicked the sentinel in the back of the left leg. The beast roared, plunged its spear down, and missed Thaddeus by an inch. Thaddeus smashed the creature in the face and it flew against the opposite shield wall. There it slithered to the earth, melting and disintegrating as it fell.

Thaddeus helped Phil to her feet. "Thank you, lass," he rumbled. "That was a brave thing."

Thaddeus turned slowly to Warren then, and his voice was flat. All laughter and vitality had left his eyes. "We've failed, lad," he said. "All is lost."

Warren stared at the mountain man but did not reply. Instead he rolled awkwardly to his feet, guarding his shattered arm, and stumbled to the shimmering shield wall. He peered at the darkness. Behind him, Ina said, "Your mother is dead."

Warren didn't turn, but remained staring out. "No," he replied. His voice was tiny and small. Barely audible.

Thaddeus stepped to Warren's side. "The devil meant to capture her," he said, nodding in Uhlgoth's direction. "But he's killed her instead." His voice was choked. "The bastard's killed her. I've no means of tellin' you how sorry I am, lad. We've failed."

"No," said Warren, slightly louder this time.

Phil and Sean stared at their friend, terrified by the words of the adults.

Warren remained focused on the shifting shapes outside the shield wall. Something new was happening out there. He heard Uhlgoth scream a muffled command and the entire Fabrinel army froze.

The red ship sank lower.

"Your mother is dead, Warren," Ina said again, louder and more firmly this time.

Warren did not respond or turn.

"What's going to happen?" cried Sean. "I mean, if all you've been saying is true …"

"Life will unravel," said Ina. "The planet will wither."

"She's not dead," said Warren, staring out.

Thaddeus and Ina glanced at each other.

"Lad," said Thaddeus gently.

"She's not dead!"

Outside, Uhlgoth stood before his frozen army and planted his feet. Shoulders back, face tilted skyward, he lifted his arms toward his ship.

"Turn the shield off," said Warren.

Thirty-eight

"Shut the shield off and move behind the ridge," said Warren. "Hurry!"

He turned to face his friends and they all saw the jagged bone jutting from his arm.

"Oh, my God, Warren," Phil cried. "Your arm."

"Please," said Warren. "I'm okay. But you have to go. Now. Turn the shield off."

"That's delirium talking, lad," rumbled Thaddeus. "You're not right in the head."

"TURN IT OFF!" Warren roared.

Lightning danced overhead and Warren's companions stepped back, even Thaddeus.

Outside, Uhlgoth stretched toward his ship, growing larger by the moment.

"Trust me!" Warren screamed. "As I've trusted you. There's no time to explain."

Thaddeus took a step toward the shield generator. Not fast enough for Warren.

The boy shut his eyes and summoned a sizzling bolt of lightning that struck the shield and cracked it like an egg. Electric current jumped and hummed.

"GET BEHIND THE RIDGE!" Warren cried, as the shield flickered like a candle and went out. "RUN!"

Thaddeus and Ina stood a moment longer. Shaken. Unsure. But then their eyes met and instantly, wordlessly, they agreed to trust the boy. A second later they were shoving Sean and Phil toward the tower and the dark meadow beyond.

All around them, Uhlgoth's soldiers stood like wax statues, leering and sinister in the red light of the descending ship.

Uhlgoth stood riveted, too, but his body was growing, quivering from head to toe as he stretched toward his ship. It flashed into Warren's mind then that Uhlgoth was like an insect on the verge of metamorphosis.

"RUN!" Warren screamed. His friends were already a hundred yards away, but it wasn't enough. "FASTER!"

The ship came lower. Uhlgoth stretched higher, and Warren dove behind the flat rock where the Eltura had placed his mother. He shielded his head with his good arm and shut his eyes tight.

There was a nuclear-bright flash and Uhlgoth's body exploded into a million flaming pieces: muscle and bone, skin and tendon, ligaments and entrails. An obscene non-sense broadcast across the meadow.

A hot, foul-smelling shockwave blasted the ridge, flattening trees and scorching the grass and bitterbrush.

Warren struggled to his feet. Fires burned here and there but Uhlgoth's frozen army looked undamaged and unchanged.

The ship came lower—a great pulsating tumor blotting out the stars.

"Mirra?" Tears of pain and terror flooded Warren eyes. "Where are you?" he whispered, afraid there might be no reply.

The ship came lower and the throbbing light changed, revealing vast metallic structures heretofore unseen. The craft was much larger than Warren had guessed. He shook violently.

"Here," whispered a voice. A soft, soothing, female voice that flowed from the ground like water from a spring.

Warren couldn't tell if he was hearing the voice or feeling it in his muscles and bones, but his terror diminished.

"You're free," said Warren.

"Yes."

Warren craned his neck and studied the monstrous ship.

"Then, Uhlgoth's failed," said the boy. "He'll leave."

"No," replied the voice. "If he can't have me, he will kill me."

Ports were opening on the ship now. Vast panels were shifting and turning, glinting in the moonlight.

"Tell me what to do," said the boy.

"Fight," whispered the voice. "Give me time."

Warren shut his eyes and the deep dark of the sky gave way to searing, blinding light. Thunder rumbled and a fantastic, zigzagging bolt split the heavens.

It was then that Warren perceived the shields.

Uhlgoth's ship was a fortress surrounded by a vast matrix of shields. Honeycomb-shaped. Separate from the body of the vessel.

The ship came lower. Apertures spun open on the underbelly of the craft and a single, skull-shattering tone rang out.

Warren could feel the vibration as the tone passed overhead like a plume of hot volcanic ash.

WHOOSH! BOOM! The fire lookout exploded off its foundation and flew a mile down ridge, flaming like a meteor.

"Fight," breathed the voice.

"Are you still my mom?" Warren cried. His arm throbbed. The pain was getting worse. "Do you ... do you know me?"

"Know you. Love you," said the gentle voice. "Always and forever. You are my son. My precious son."

Warren shut his eyes. Thunder rumbled and another fantastic bolt cut the sky. Lightning. Seventeen thousand degrees. Hotter than the surface of the sun. This bolt hit Uhlgoth's shields, illuminating the vast honeycomb structure but causing not the slightest bit of damage.

The ship came lower. More apertures unwound. And another clear tone—this one ten thousand times more powerful than the last—vomited forth, bound for Mt. Constance.

Nine thousand foot Constance was the nearest Cascade peak. Warren could see it across the valley; majestic snow covered flanks glimmering in the moonlight. He'd climbed Constance with his uncle.

The sound weapon smashed the peak like God's fist, shearing off the top three thousand feet in a single, cataclysmic blow.

A thousand hydrogen bombs could not have done more damage, and the roar that ensued built into a furious cacophony of crashing, avalanching ice and stone. It shook the earth for a hundred miles in every direction.

The sound weapon's deadly tone faded into a monotonous, low-frequency hum, and Warren gawked stupidly at the gaping black nothingness where the peak had been.

Uhlgoth was invincible. His rage boundless. Denied his prize, he now wanted only to torture Gaia before obliterating her.

The sound weapon would split the planet in two. Warren knew this in his exhausted, battered bones.

Thirty-nine

"Filthy mongrel!" Uhlgoth roared, suddenly leaping like a demon into Warren's weakened mind; ramming his way in with the force of a sledgehammer.

Warren cried out, crumpled to his knees and felt his connection with Gaia breaking.

"You dare confront me, boy?"

Sheets of lightning lit up the sky, blasting the far side of the ridge where Thaddeus and the others were hiding. Uhlgoth was usurping Warren's power to kill his friends.

"Filthy mongrel!" screamed Uhlgoth, pushing hard to sever the connection between Warren and his mother. "You can't fight me!"

"You can," whispered the other voice, as Warren's head sagged and his strength evaporated. "You must."

"You'll die here," sneered Uhlgoth. "Just as your father died. Weak and helpless."

Warren let his body sag further, let Uhlgoth believe he was giving up; then suddenly pushed back with all his might. It was a desperate move. If he couldn't shove the demon from his mind now he'd never be able to. His strength was nearly gone.

The move worked. Warren staggered to his feet and instantly summoned a new barrage of lightning.

Fresh bolts scorched Uhlgoth's shields from all sides. Lightning lit up the meadows and Uhlgoth's eerie statue army like the noonday sun.

Warren staggered. The beast was gone from his mind but its sudden attack had hurt him terribly. Gaia's vast power surged beneath his feet but he was losing the ability to channel it. His exhausted body was giving out.

Uhlgoth's power, on the other hand, had redoubled. More ports were spinning open on the underbelly of the ship.

Warren concentrated, drawing bolt after bolt from the ionosphere, hurling them against the honeycomb shields with his mind, like molten spears.

He paused to gasp for breath, and heard the sound weapon cycling up, whining like a colossal assembly line machine pushed far beyond capacity.

DROOM! DROOM! DROOM! Tight knots of sound whickered past Warren's head, slamming into the ridge and detonating like cruise missiles.

The disparate tones built, unified, and coalesced into a single note. And now the entire underbelly of the craft was opening, stretching wide. The death-blow was coming.

Warren caused another furious lightning barrage, and this time he glimpsed a shape rising behind the red ship.

Towering. Black. Ominous.

"What is that?" he gasped, as darkness swallowed the sky once more. "What's happening?"

A jagged slab of rock wound past Warren's head, just missing him. A huge old growth tree roared by, spinning like a propeller. And now Warren was drowning in an ocean of sudden sound. Uhlgoth was unleashing his entire arsenal at once.

"Hit him," came the voice, and Warren conjured a final, fantastically powerful bolt. Born miles up in the deep dark, it fractured the June sky, switch-backing through the atmosphere until it stabbed Uhlgoth's shields like a flaming, razor tipped sword.

The flash revealed the mysterious black tower once more, just for an instant, and suddenly Warren understood.

Gaia had summoned a funnel cloud. A colossal, steadily advancing twister, larger than any the world had ever seen.

Gravel raked Warren's head and arms, and the earth shook.

Uhlgoth hadn't seen the twister yet, so intent was he on killing, and on repelling Warren's lightning.

The sound weapon punched the ground and slit the earth's crust like a scalpel. A ten-mile-long fissure cut the ridge and the sound tore deeper.

Then the sound warped abruptly, and Warren felt Uhlgoth's sudden terror.

A rumble erupted from the darkness behind the ship.

The rumble became a roar.

The ship lifted. Tried to flee. But the twister was already brushing it.

The honeycomb shields vibrated.

The vessel rose.

Two seconds more and it would clear the storm.

Power plants flared. Thrusters fired. Drives hummed.

Too late.

The shields blinked, wobbled, and gave way.

Warren stared. For an instant, the great ship hung there, twinkling like an ornament. Then it spun hard and leapt laterally toward the roaring buzz-saw of the tornado, disintegrating as it fell.

Great luminous panels buckled and exploded. House-sized molten red disks twisted, warped and detonated. Neon-blue liquid accreted around the spinning juggernaut like Saturn's rings, then vanished inside.

The shrieking, roaring, mile-tall funnel cloud hung there in the dark, digesting the ship with a steady roar, ripping and pureeing it into a billion tiny bits.

Lightning flashed and Warren saw with dismay that the rampaging twister was moving again.

I should run, he thought. But he had not the strength.

"Lie down," came the soothing voice, and Warren staggered and collapsed into the grass. He lay there, too exhausted to move, gazing out through a veil of light—the same light Todd Jr. had seen enveloping Mirra in the forest, hours earlier.

The tornado raged above Warren, raining bits of Uhlgoth's obliterated ship over the ridge, spewing fountains of shrapnel like confetti. But the boy felt safe inside the veil, detached from the mayhem of the storm. Warren's eyelids grew heavier, the roar fainter, and all at once he was aware that the horrible, throbbing pain had left his arm. He drifted to sleep, wondering if he had died.

Forty

When Warren awoke he was lying on his back, staring at the sky. It was peaceful. Cloudless. Pale blue. The air was cool and it was quiet; so quiet Warren wondered for a moment if he'd gone deaf during the battle. Then a bird called softly in the distance, and he sighed, relieved. It was, he guessed, an hour before sunrise.

"You must be hungry," said a familiar voice.

Warren blinked, stretched and turned to find Phil and Sean sitting in the grass watching him. They looked as if they'd been dragged cross country by galloping horses, but their faces were bright and smiling. Warren had never been so happy to see anyone.

"You guys look terrible," he laughed. He sat up slowly, instinctively guarding his shattered arm.

"Not as bad as you," said Sean. "How's the arm?"

Warren studied his arm and gently made a fist, expecting a shock of pain. There was no pain. Even more amazing, the jutting bone had settled back into proper position. He touched the skin with his fingertips. There was no sign of a wound or damage.

"I don't understand," he whispered.

Sean smiled. "What else is new?"

"It's okay?" asked Phil. "Your arm?"

"Yeah."

"Have a donut," she said. And she presented Warren with a box of white powdered donuts.

Warren stared at the box, then at Phil. "Where'd this come from?"

"Fire loof-out" said Sean, his mouth crammed with food. Phil regarded him with mild disgust.

"There's crates of stuff smashed all over the ridge down that way," Sean waved. "Thaddeus found it."

"Where is Thaddeus?" Warren asked. He sat up straighter and dug into a donut. It tasted better than any donut he'd ever eaten.

"He and Ina," said Phil, pulling her hair into a ponytail, "are running around the ridge, smashing pieces of the ship so the US Army doesn't get it."

Warren stood and saw that he had not dreamed the events of the previous night. The ridge sparkled with debris from Uhlgoth's obliterated craft.

"Doesn't look like there's much left to smash," he said.

Patches of forest below the meadows had burned; the result of lightning or flaming debris. But there was no fire now. Only blackened trees. It had been a wet spring, thankfully. Far more shocking than the burned trees was a gaping fissure, perhaps twenty-five feet wide, just below the crest of the ridge, running as far as Warren could see in both directions.

"It's deep," said Sean. "Can't even see the bottom in most places. I don't know how we'll get across it."

"He was trying to cut the planet in half," whispered Warren, as memories of the battle with Uhlgoth flooded back.

Warren turned to the west and his breath left him. Snow covered Mt. Constance was gone. All that remained was a great stump; a grey plateau, smoking forlornly in the early light. The mountain had been blown off its foundation. Warren wondered how many thousands of acres of trees, lakes, streams and trails had been obliterated.

"Your mom is okay then?" Phil asked.

"Yeah," said Warren. The fearsome, raging power he'd felt the night before had settled into a steady, rhythmic heartbeat, but he could feel the rhythm in his bones, feel his mother's presence. "She's here. She's alive."

"But how?" said Sean, looking slightly ridiculous with white donut frosting encrusting his filthy chin. "I thought, I mean … Ina told us that in order for Onatah to go free, someone had to sing."

"Someone did," rumbled a deep voice.

The children turned to see Thaddeus stepping quickly through the grass. He was carrying a small, blood-spattered form in his arms.

The big man knelt and carefully laid the body on the soft earth. It was clearly a child, or young teenager, but the face was unfamiliar. At first.

"Oh my God," gasped Phil. "It's Todd Jr."

It *was* Todd Jr., yet not the same boy they knew from school. The loud-mouthed bully was gone, replaced by a gaunt, hollow-cheeked child with skin the color of rotting cheese. Bloody gashes covered his face, arms and torso.

"Aye," rumbled Thaddeus, "it's him." He gently lifted Junior's forearm to take his pulse. "And a fearless lad he is. We owe him everything."

The children stared at one another, too stunned to speak.

Warren sucked in his breath. And though he didn't understand, though his mind was jammed with a thousand sudden questions, the loathing and contempt he'd always felt for Todd Finley Jr. melted away in an instant.

"He sang to her?" Warren asked.

"Aye."

"But how? What …"

"Hush," Thaddeus whispered. He released Junior's arm and got to his feet. Then he beckoned the children to a spot a few feet away.

"He's hanging by a thread," said the big man. "Could die at any moment and there's naught I can do to help him."

"But you said Marines were coming," said Sean. "FBI, Park Service."

"In droves, true," said Thaddeus. "But not soon enough. His injuries are grave."

"But …"

"Hush," Thaddeus said again. And he fixed his gaze on Warren. "He wants to talk to you."

"Me?"

"Yes. The three of us will step away."

Warren stared helplessly as his friends retreated. Phil brushed away a flood of sudden tears, so pitiful did Junior look.

Warren stepped to Junior's side, knelt slowly, and surveyed the boy's wounds. Junior's chest rose and fell with a broken, painful wheeze.

"I'm sorry," Todd Jr. whispered. His eyes had not opened, but somehow he knew Warren was there.

"It's okay," said Warren, tears unexpectedly welling in his own eyes.

"If I hadn't stolen the medallion," Junior hissed. "If ..." He choked on the words and coughed up drops of bright red blood.

Warren took his hand. "It's okay," he said earnestly. "Thaddeus says you saved everything."

Todd Jr.'s eyes flashed open and he regarded Warren with sudden focus and intensity.

"I know about the treasure," he said.

"Treasure?"

"It's not gold. Not like that." Junior coughed up more blood and his voice grew hoarse.

"Don't try to talk," said Warren. "Help is coming."

Junior ignored him. "Angel's Arch. You know it?"

Warren nodded. "Sure. Yeah. I've been there."

Angel's arch was a natural stone arch, one of the most visited backpacker destinations in the North Cascades. It sat in deep forest at the base of Clearwater Ridge, roughly five miles from their current location.

"The arch opens onto a Center Point."

Warren wondered if Junior was losing his grip on reality. "A Center Point?"

"The Mendari ..." Junior hissed, staring at Warren with fierce, unblinking eyes. "They knew Europeans were settling back east. Knew they'd move west. Knew the Denelai would be obliterated."

Junior's breath was coming in gasps now.

"Don't talk," said Warren. "Just breathe. Everything's gonna be okay."

"The Mendari loved the Denelai," Junior continued, as if he hadn't even heard Warren. "Wanted to help them. Give them an escape route. At the arch."

Warren had no idea what the boy was talking about.

"Take the medallion," Junior gasped, as he lifted his hand to his blood-soaked vest. "Don't let anyone else find the Center Point."

Junior's eyes went wide and he erupted in a fit of violent, rattling coughs. It sounded like his chest was breaking.

"It's okay," said Warren, and he clutched Junior's hand. "Help is coming. Army medics." He turned to his friends. "Thaddeus!" he called. "Come quick!"

When he turned back, Junior had stopped breathing and blood was oozing from the corner of his mouth. His eyes were wide. Staring.

"Thaddeus!"

The big man knelt beside him and felt for the pulse in Junior's neck.

"Do something!" Warren cried. "CPR! We can do CPR until help gets here!"

"Naught can be done," said Thaddeus gently. "He's dead. It's a wonder he held on as long as he did."

Forty-one

They covered Junior's body with a blanket from the fire lookout, and Phil placed a bouquet of wildflowers—held together with one of her hair bands—at his side. Ina rejoined the group and they stood together in silence. Tears flowed.

"The world will never truly appreciate what happened here," said Thaddeus, after a long while. "What really happened."

Warren glanced at the big man and saw that his head was bowed. Eyes shut.

"But humankind owes this boy a debt of gratitude all the same. He did the right thing. He did the hard and difficult thing. He stood against his own flesh and blood when he knew it had gone evil. And his selfless bravery averted calamity. We shall not forget."

Silence followed Thaddeus's words. Silence and more tears.

"Children," Thaddeus said at last, and the group seemed to breathe once again. "We need to talk."

He beckoned them to sit in the grass and they arranged themselves around him. He looked each one in the eye.

"Helicopters are coming," he said. "Soldiers on foot, also. From every direction. You have only to sit here and wait for rescue."

"What about you?" said Sean.

"We don't want to be rescued," said Ina.

"You're leaving?"

"Aye," said Thaddeus.

"But where will you go?" asked Warren. "When will we see you again?"

Thaddeus started to answer, then muttered something unintelligible and turned away. He brushed his face with one massive forearm and Warren wondered if he was crying. It was an unnerving thought.

"We will go ... away," said Ina. "And you will not see us again. Ever."

"What?" Warren cried. "Why not? We could meet sometime. After the army leaves, after ..."

"Our work is finished," said Thaddeus, and tears welled in his ancient gray eyes. "Your mother is free. Safe."

"Yes, but ..."

"Enough," said Ina, and she rose quickly to her feet. The others did the same.

"Thaddeus and I must get under cover. Now."

Ina removed the medallion from her pocket. She'd taken it from Todd Jr.'s vest and cleansed it of blood and dirt. Warren hadn't had the heart to remove it, but he stared at the relic now.

The gold and jewels flashed in the morning light.

"This is yours as much as anyone's," said Ina, handing the medallion to Warren. "Though how you will keep it from the authorities I cannot guess. They will want to know everything. Examine everything."

Warren took the medallion and jammed it quickly into a pocket, but Ina glanced at the sky and smiled. "No good," she said. "They've already seen it. Satellites, you know."

"The things that happened here," said Thaddeus, "have shaken the planet."

Sean looked at the immense gash in the ridge and the distant, smoking base of Mt. Constance. "Literally," he muttered.

"All eyes are trained here," said Thaddeus. "The authorities want answers."

"You will be famous," said Ina. "World famous. Though they may find some of your stories hard to believe."

Phil burst into tears. "I don't want to be famous. I just want to go home."

"Courage, lass," rumbled Thaddeus. "You will go home, by day's end, I've little doubt. Goodbye."

Warren stammered, upset. "I can't believe you're leaving ... just like that."

"We must," said Thaddeus. "And you must go home."

Warren stared at him, then turned and faced the deepest, wildest part of the park; a region of rugged, inaccessible valleys and jagged, snow covered peaks. "This *is* my home," he whispered.

Thaddeus smiled, then pulled the boy aside. "Lad. Listen to me."

Warren waited as Thaddeus composed his thoughts.

"You've done well."

"Thanks."

"You came into this knowin' little to nothing of your real history. And you've handled the truth like a man. Better then most men would've."

Warren didn't know what to say.

"You've shown courage and compassion in fine balance, and I believe if anyone can handle the pressure that's to come, you can."

"Pressure?" said Warren, confused.

"Lad," said Thaddeus, lowering his voice and clasping Warren's shoulder. "You are your Mother's son. Your power will grow. Temptations will arise. Terrible temptations. Show restraint, lad. Humility. Always."

"I'll try," said Warren.

Thaddeus released Warren from his grip, satisfied.

"Goodbye, Warren Wilkes," said Ina, fixing the boy with the same sharp, critical gaze she'd used at Ridgecrest. "You did okay. Better than I imagined possible when we first met."

"Thanks," said Warren. "I think."

Ina smiled and hugged him. And with that, she and Thaddeus turned and walked toward the chasm as the children watched. Twenty feet from the edge, they began to jog. The jog turned into a sprint, and when they hit the lip of the massive fissure, they kicked off hard, leaping into the air like Olympic long jumpers.

"What's a Center Point?" Warren cried, rushing to the edge of the chasm.

Thaddeus and Ina crashed to earth on the far side of the gap and turned hard in the dirt.

"A myth!" Ina shouted. "Where did you hear the term?"

"Todd Jr. told me the medallion leads to a Center Point," Warren yelled. "At Angel's Arch. He said the Center Point *is* the treasure. What does it mean?"

To the children's surprise, Ina and Thaddeus leapt immediately back across the chasm.

"It means you need to give me the medallion," said Ina, as she slammed into the dirt next to Warren. She extended her hand. "Now. Please."

Warren handed her the glittering relic. "But you said we won't see you again."

"You won't. Goodbye."

"So you're gonna find the treasure yourselves then? Or whatever it is?"

"No," Thaddeus replied. "We're going to destroy the relic."

Warren was stunned. "What? Why?"

"Cannot risk the authorities finding a Center Point," said the big man. "Unthinkable mayhem could come of it."

Ina was already jogging toward the chasm again and now Thaddeus was turning as well.

"Take me there!" Warren cried.

Thaddeus and Ina wheeled impatiently. All at once they could hear the rhythmic *WHUMP! WHUMP! WHUMP!* of helicopters at the southern end of the valley.

"No time!" Thaddeus cried. "I'm sorry, lad."

"But Angel's Arch is close!" Warren yelled. "The same direction you're going. We could see the Center Thing or whatever it's called, and you could just leave me there."

"THERE IS NO TIME!" Ina screamed.

"But …"

"They've seen you," said Thaddeus, gesturing at the sky. "They will not let us pass without a skirmish, and we've no wish for that."

There was a power well nearby. Warren had sensed it earlier. He leapt to it now and shut his eyes. "I can give us cover," he said.

"Cover?" Thaddeus squinted at him.

"Please!" Warren shouted.

"What d'ya mean, *cover*?"

The group stared at Warren, who'd gone as still as a stone pillar.

"Look!" Phil cried.

Wisps of fog floated from the forest canopy below. The wisps grew thicker, denser by the moment. Fog rose from the chasm, too, and as they watched, crooked fingers of fog crept from the forest edge. Another wall of clouds rolled over the ridge above, tumbling like a slow-motion wave down to meet them.

"Please," Warren begged, opening his eyes. The helicopters were getting louder.

"You don't really want to destroy the relic. You want to see the treasure, too. I know it."

"Damn you!" Thaddeus cried.

With a grunt, he lunged at the boy, seized him by the shirt, and threw him over his shoulder like a sack of dog food. Then he turned and sprinted for the chasm once more. Warren shut his eyes and clutched Thaddeus's hide coat for dear life as the mountain man kicked off.

"Wait!" screamed Phil, as they crashed to the ground. She and Sean were still on the other side. "We want to come, too! We have to stay together!"

The helicopters—an armada of green US Army ships—were almost on top of them. But the fog was closing in as well.

"Damn you all!" Thaddeus roared, and with another grunt he threw Warren roughly to the ground and leapt back across the abyss.

Warren got to his feet to find Ina glaring at him.

"The Finleys' lawyer was right, Warren Wilkes. You are a born troublemaker. They should have thrown you in jail."

Thaddeus crashed to earth with Phil draped over one shoulder and Sean over the other, and shook them off as unceremoniously as he'd discarded Warren.

Swirling fog enveloped them, dramatically dimming the bright morning light and making the world suddenly gray and soft. The chasm now looked alien and mysterious, and it was hard to see much detail beyond the far rim.

"Keep your mouths shut and keep pace," said Thaddeus irritably, his tangled beard suddenly festooned with glistening water droplets. He turned and bounded down slope with Ina at his side and the children careening after.

Forty-two

"What is a Center Point?" gasped Warren, after fifteen minutes of steady running and speed-hiking.

At first they'd jumped and tumbled steeply down slope, through open meadow. To the children—trying desperately to keep up—Thaddeus and Ina resembled ghosts vanishing into the fog ahead.

Warren knew the adults were not running full out, just fast enough to make the journey difficult and uncomfortable. He didn't think the adults would abandon them—a couple of times he thought he saw Thaddeus glance back to check on their whereabouts—but he didn't want to find out.

Once in the forest, the pace slowed considerably. Thaddeus was making a beeline for Angel's Arch, Warren knew, and there was no direct trail. They were cutting cross-country, moving as quickly and quietly as possible through deep forest.

Twice they'd heard the rumble of heavy transport helicopters high overhead. And once they heard shouting, and bursts of radio chatter, perhaps a quarter of a mile away, to the east.

"A Center Point," came Thaddeus's whispered reply, "is a place. A sort of ... terminal."

"What? Like an airport terminal?" said Phil, as she vaulted gracefully over a huge fallen tree. The behemoth, moss-covered log stretched like a lonely highway into the grey gloom.

"More like a train terminal, lass," Thaddeus replied. "With tracks leading out from the station in different directions. Like spokes on a wheel."

"Can't be at Angel's Arch," said Sean. "I've been there. Climbed all over it. Thousands of people have. Maybe tens of thousands."

"Don't be so sure, lad," said Thaddeus. "Many a thing exists that cannot be seen with the plain eye. The medallion ..."

He froze mid sentence and mid stride. "Down!" he hissed, and the children dropped instantly into the moss and ferns. Ina dove to the left and rolled to her feet, knife ready. Thaddeus's knife was out now, too, and the great blade glinted in the fog.

Warren lifted his head, and gasped. Phil followed his gaze and stifled a scream.

There was a Blank Frame standing under a tree, thirty feet ahead. It was staring at them.

"Satan's spawn," Thaddeus hissed, as threads of fluorescent green laser light burst from his left eye. The threads formed a twinkling green pyramid a couple of feet in front of his face, alive with shapes and symbols. After a couple of seconds the pyramid blinked off.

"Blank Frame in stasis," reported Thaddeus, relaxing a bit.

"I count thirty-two survivors," said Ina, examining her own neon-bright projection.

As the children watched, Thaddeus tipped his great knife with a dot of cyber toxin from his tortoise shell box, strode straight to the motionless, wide-eyed Fabrinel, and stabbed the creature in the heart. The soldier's face melted, like wax in a furnace. Then the rest of its body sagged, collapsed and imploded, disintegrating into nothingness.

"Make that thirty-one," rumbled Thaddeus, as he wiped his knife clean on some moss.

The children were on their feet again. "Thirty-one?" said Sean. "You mean there are thirty-one more like that?"

"Aye," Thaddeus replied. "In stasis."

"What's *stasis*?"

"Shut off. Uhlgoth shut them down during the battle to protect them from the sound weapon."

"But how did the Fabrinel get here?" asked Phil.

Ina stared at a patch of fog enveloping a tangle of immense, fallen trees. As if on cue, the fog receded, just enough to reveal another Blank. This one lay on top of a huge root ball, stiff as a department store mannequin.

"The tornado must've picked 'em up off the ridge," said Thaddeus. "Scattered 'em here."

Ina leapt like a cat onto the root mass and dispatched the prone Fabrinel with her own glowing knife.

Fog swirled around the group, advancing and retreating like the tide.

"Nice," hissed Sean, and Warren followed his gaze.

Sixty feet to the east was yet another Fabrinel Blank. This one protruded like an arrow from the trunk of a mammoth, old growth Douglas Fir. The creature's head and shoulders were buried inside the tree, but the body stuck straight out, like a diving board. Perpendicular to the trunk.

"How fast do you have to be going to be impaled in a tree?" whispered Sean.

"*Dorothy!*" said Warren, imitating a character from *The Wizard of Oz*.

"Who is *Dorothy*?" Thaddeus asked irritably. He furrowed his great bushy eyebrows at the boy.

"Oh, um ..." said Warren. "Never mind."

Warren remembered reading about Midwest twisters; fantastically powerful storms that carried debris for miles. He remembered seeing a picture of an old vinyl record embedded in the bark of an elm tree, hurled with such force and velocity that it pierced the bark like a knife. Warren was fairly certain this was the first time Mother Nature had stabbed a tree with a robot from another galaxy.

Thaddeus's pyramid hologram snapped suddenly back on. "US Army patrols closing on us," he said. "They've seen the children."

"How?" said Warren, looking around. The fog was thick.

"Thermal imaging," said Thaddeus. "We aren't the only ones with fancy tools."

Ina considered the news for a moment. "Take the children to the Arch," she told Thaddeus. "Destroy the three Fabrinels in your path, and I'll take care of the rest. Go."

"Aye," whispered Thaddeus, nodding. "See you at the arch."

He looked at the children. "Stay together. Stay close to me. Stay quiet."

Warren turned to say goodbye to Ina, but she was already twenty feet up a Douglas Fir tree, climbing fast, a glowing knife clenched firmly in her teeth. She looked like a pirate stealing aboard a ship.

Warren craned his neck and saw her target: another Blank Frame tangled in the uppermost branches of the great tree. Fog swallowed the canopy, Ina vanished from sight, and Warren turned and followed Thaddeus and the others.

He would not see Ina again.

Forty-three

Thaddeus and the children hurried on through the woods. Three times, as they waded through dense fog, they came upon Blank Frames scattered by the twister. The shock of encountering the creatures in the constantly shifting mist never wore off.

On one occasion, only the Fabrinel's pale face was visible. It gazed up at them from a deep forest pool where it had evidently landed.

Thaddeus knelt, raised the creature's dripping body with his stump arm, and stabbed it with his knife. The creature collapsed with a sigh, sank back into the black water and vanished. Warren and the others shivered and followed Thaddeus as he moved on.

"Why do you have to kill them?" asked Phil.

Thaddeus grunted. "Lass," he said, "Fabrinels are at least a thousand years beyond earthly science craft. Imagine what could happen if the US Army got hold of a Blank Frame and started tinkering with it?"

He paused as another Blank became visible through the mist, this one leaning like a statue against a fallen tree. Thaddeus lifted it. Stabbed it through the chest.

"Imagine if the Army switched it on, by accident," he said, wiping his knife clean. "Worse yet, imagine if some crafty Army egghead unlocked its secrets and made more."

"An invincible army," mused Sean. "The ultimate weapon."

"Aye," said Thaddeus dryly, "and you've enough of those already."

"So that's it?" asked Phil, after Thaddeus had destroyed the third Blank. "If Ina kills the rest of the survivors, that means there are no more of Uhlgoth's machines, anywhere on the planet?"

"Correct," replied Thaddeus.

"No more Fabrinels?" Phil continued. "I mean …" she stammered and turned red. "You know, besides, um …"

"Beside Ina and me, lass, that's right. We are what we are. No need to sugar coat things."

"So then …" Phil pointed to the tortoise shell box in Thaddeus's jacket pocket. "You won't need that stuff anymore, will you? The cyber toxin?"

Thaddeus peered at her through narrowed eyes, glanced at the box, and muttered something unintelligible. Then he turned and climbed over a fallen log.

"I mean," Phil said, "if the enemy Fabrinels are really all dead, or dissolved, or whatever … you can get rid of it. Right? It's dangerous to carry around."

Thaddeus pressed on, moving like a panther through

the deep forest. He didn't answer or look back, so Phil hurried to catch him. Warren and Sean were twenty feet behind.

"Unless you *are* planning to use the toxin again," she whispered. "For something else."

Thaddeus stopped and spun hard. "Lass," he growled. "What're ya drivin' at? Be out with it."

Warren and Sean halted at a respectful distance.

"You *are* planning to use it again, aren't you?" Phil whispered. "You and Ina. On yourselves."

The mountain man saw tears in Phil's eyes and his demeanor softened. "Now lass," he rumbled. "What could have planted such a thought in that head a yers?"

"The way Ina said you were 'going away,'" said Phil miserably. "That we wouldn't see you again. Ever."

"Aw, girlie …"

"Please. Just tell me the truth. Will you use it? The toxin? On yourself?"

Thaddeus stared at her, and his ancient eyes glinted like jewels in the diffuse light. "Our work," he said, "is done. We've a right to go."

Phil held his gaze. "But that's … that's … suicide."

"It's dyin', is what it is, child," said Thaddeus. "Powerful little can hurt a Fabrinel, as you've witnessed. But we've a right to die, same as anyone. When our time is up."

"But how do you know when your time is up?"

Thaddeus laughed. "Lass, my time was up four and a half centuries ago. I died that day, flesh and blood, but agreed to stay on to protect Onatah and see her home safe and sound. I've kept my end of the bargain." He started moving again, and Phil stayed close.

"But why do you want to go?" she whispered, as Thaddeus helped her over an enormous fallen tree.

"I'm weary, girl," he replied.

"I thought you didn't get tired."

"Not bone weary, *soul* weary." He touched his chest. "My soul is original. The only part of me that is. It was here when I was flesh and blood and it's still here now and it needs a rest.

"Also, lass, grateful as I am to the Mendari for this …" he gestured at his body; "… frame of mine; marvelous as it is, it ain't a proper body. This ain't really living." Thaddeus stared at her so hard she thought he was looking through her.

"I remember what it was like …" he said wistfully. "Kissing my beautiful wife and holding her near." Phil blushed.

"The warmth of the fire. The feel of winter's icy blast on my cheeks.

"I remember being hungry. And that first taste of fresh-killed venison off the spit. The smell of coffee."

"You don't have those things now?" Phil asked. "Taste and stuff?"

Thaddeus laughed. "Girlie, I've eaten naught but sunlight for four hundred years. Wondrous efficient method of sustenance, but bloody damn dull. I'm not a plant."

He looked at the ground and his voice cracked with anguish. "My people, all the people that loved me, child, are dead. Dead and turned to dust ages ago. It's time I followed them home."

"Thank you," Phil said quietly, as they moved on. "For explaining."

Thaddeus shrugged.

"A lot of adults would never have done that."

The big man made no reply.

"Can I say two things, though?" Phil asked softly, after a couple of minutes.

Thaddeus looked at her and she touched his arm.

"If you don't feel, why do you cry sometimes?"

"You're mistaken," he growled. "I do not cry. I cannot."

"Yeah. Whatever."

"You said *two* things," he said irritably. "What's the other?"

Phil looked the giant in the eye, then glanced back at Sean and Warren.

"You said that the people who loved you are dead and gone." Tears welled in Phil's eyes and her voice trembled. "Not all of them, Thaddeus. Not all of them."

Forty-four

Angel's Arch appeared through the swirling fog like the gateway to a mythical city. Twenty-nine feet tall, the stone arch graced a remote, heavily-forested valley deep in the mountains. It spanned hurrying Angel Creek and a trail known as the Staircase, and was a popular year-round destination for sightseers, photographers and geology buffs.

"I've been here lots of times," whispered Warren, as he halted amid the ferns and absorbed the scene before them. "But I've never seen it like this."

Dense tentacles of fog embraced the elegant stone span, silently seizing and releasing the rock, curling and uncurling, shifting and drifting around and under and over it in ever changing patterns.

"What's different?" asked Phil, who'd never visited and was simultaneously awed and frightened. The arch looked mysterious in the half-light, like the last intact structure in an unexplored ruin. "Just the fog?

"No," said Warren. "There are always other people." He pointed to a small clearing near the arch's western base. "Usually a tent or two over there. Someone climbing around."

Thaddeus's right eye pitched forward in its socket and a small, rectangular hologram, painfully bright in the gloom, flashed on. He spoke as if sharing an interesting tidbit from the newspaper. "There are only three back-packers, two fishermen and one gold-panner left in the entire two million acre park," he said. "And they're all dead."

"Great," muttered Sean.

"What about military?" said Warren. "The guys tracking us?"

"Less than two miles out and closing. *Carefully*. If you've still a mind to try the relic, you'd best be about it."

"What about Ina?" Phil asked.

Thaddeus scanned another part of the shimmering rectangle. "She's destroyed all of Uhlgoth's Blank Frames except two, and she's hunting those now. Don't worry about Ina. She'll find us."

Warren removed the medallion from his pocket and stepped forward. A memory leapt to mind as he did so—a memory long hidden and buried—of his first visit to the arch. In the memory, he was very small, and he was with his mom and dad. It was winter and he was riding in a pack on his dad's back. That was all he could recollect, except … feelings. Powerful feelings, of joy, love, happiness.

He looked around. His mother was near now, watching him. Concerned about him. All these years he'd believed he was alone. But he was not alone, and the relief and contentment he gained from that knowledge was indescribable. His mother was here now. Close at hand. Except ...

"Thaddeus," Warren whispered.

"Aye?"

"There are power-wells here, approaching the arch. Circling it."

"Aye."

"Onatah's here. All around us. Only ..."

"Only, what?"

"Only, not *next* to the arch. Not under it. It's like ..." Warren squinted as if trying to see something hidden beneath the great rock span. "It's like there's a wall around this place." He struggled for a better description. "It's separated somehow. I can't explain it."

Thaddeus looked troubled, as if he'd just remembered something unpleasant. "An island," he muttered, mostly to himself.

"What?" said Sean. "*What's* an island?"

"This ground," said Thaddeus, gesturing at the arch and the space around it. "The Denelai whispered as much." He scanned the children's faces. "The arch is sacred. Was to the First People, anyway. Folks camping 'neath it and climbin' on it; throw the elders into a murderous fit of rage, it would."

Sean turned bright red at this. He'd climbed on the arch numerous times.

"Denelai were forbidden from even walking beneath it," Thaddeus continued. "Bad medicine. Very bad. Warriors journeyed here and left offerings at the base."

"But how is it like an island?" asked Phil.

"The Denelai believed it weren't part of The Firmament."

Sean snorted. "What's that supposed to mean? The arch isn't part of the Earth?"

"Correct."

"Well what is it then?"

"Something different. Older. It's hinted at in the Denelai songs. The old stories."

"It's an Indian myth."

"Aye. But so's the Center Point, lad. Only a myth. And yet here we are."

He leaned closer. "And hold this in your mind: the geologists can't fathom it either." He waved at the arch. "The rock don't match the surroundings. It don't fit. Oh, the eggheads have come up with all nature of theories and prognostications, all right." He grunted. "None of 'em worth a drop of rancid spittle."

Phil grimaced at the description and the big man nodded at Warren, urging him forward. "Be on with it, lad. Try the relic. We haven't much time."

"But how?" said Warren, lifting the medallion and holding it like a compass. "Where? The arch is huge."

"I've no idea, boy," growled Thaddeus. "All's I know for certain sure is that you're running out of time."

Warren stepped forward and with each pace felt the connection to his mother fade. The ground around the arch *was* like an island; somehow *on*the Earth, yet not *of* the Earth. Gaia was anxiously watching him from the edge, telling him to be careful.

"I will," said Warren out loud.

"You will what?" said Sean, who was right beside him.

"Oh, um, nothing."

"Tell us what Todd Jr. said," urged Phil. "Before he died. What did he say about the medallion?"

Warren thought for a moment. "He said the Mendari knew that the Denelai were about to be overrun by white settlers, people moving west. The Mendari loved the Denelai and wanted to give them an escape route. A place to go.

"A Center Point," said Phil.

They were almost under the arch now and the massive span was slick and wet from the fog.

"Yeah," said Warren. "Junior said the Center Point *was* the treasure."

"If it truly is a Center Point," said Thaddeus, "it'd be worth an ocean of gold. Try the medallion, boy. Hurry."

Warren held the relic aloft and stepped away from the group. The icon gleamed, brighter than normal. It seemed to be generating its own light now, not just reflecting it. The seven blue gems sparkled and the relic's black obsidian heart glinted like a mirror.

Warren stepped closer to the arch and lifted the relic higher. The medallion blazed like a tiny sun now, a sun with a perfect black hole at its core. Mist swirled around Warren, so thick he could almost drink it. Fog caressed the deep green forest on all sides and the oxygen-saturated air was like a feast, a delicious, satisfying meal that heightened awareness and sharpened the mind.

Warren sensed his friends behind him and could feel their anticipation. But there was another source of tension here he couldn't define. An inexplicable feeling of watchfulness and foreboding; as if the trees and rocks themselves were waiting to see what Warren Wilkes would do.

Warren stepped into the archway and—still holding the relic high—placed his thumb on its obsidian core.

Nothing happened. No electric shock. No pictures in his mind's eye. The stream at his feet continued to chatter and the fog continued to swirl. He could hear his friends breathing.

Alarm gripped Warren. If the relic needed to be placed … positioned in a certain spot …

He remembered how Mr. Finley had labored for hours before Todd Jr. accidentally discovered the gap between the stones. Warren and his friends didn't have hours. People were looking for them. People were coming.

Warren slowly scanned the arch, from one base to the other, concentrating. There was no obvious place to position the relic.

He traced the arch again, and this time fixed his gaze on a familiar object near the span's eastern foundation. It was an object that had always fascinated Warren and his uncle.

"I wonder …" he said.

The object in question was a sheared-off column of stone, approximately three feet high. The remarkable thing about "The Pedestal," as Warren and his uncle called it, was that it looked exactly like the base of another arch: same dimensions, same type and color of stone. The smooth surface of "The Pedestal" was even angled the right way.

Warren remembered asking his uncle if there had, in fact, been two arches at some time in the distant past.

"Very observant," Dave Wilkes had said to him. "And you're not the first to ask. Geologists studying the arch way back in the 1920s wondered the same thing. It sure looks like the base for another arch—one that broke and fell apart. But they couldn't find any evidence of such a thing."

Geological proof notwithstanding, Warren continued to wonder about the pedestal whenever they hiked by. And it drew his attention now.

As his friends watched, he stepped to the stone and dangled the medallion over it.

"Hellfire," Thaddeus muttered, as the relic leapt from the boy's hand with a whir.

To Warren it felt as if a powerful magnet had jerked the icon from his grasp. Instead of flying into the stone and sticking there, however, the relic stopped in mid air, two feet over the middle of the pedestal, and began slowly spinning.

"Just like at the boulders," Sean whispered.

"Yeah," said Warren.

"The medallion's getting brighter," said Phil. "You can barely look at it."

She was right. The relic was blazing now like an emergency flare, lighting up the dark forest and chasing away the shadows. All except Thaddeus shielded their eyes or looked away. But Warren saw that the light contained many colors. Blue rays stabbed from the fiery gems like blue lightning, and gold light shot from the body of the spinning relic like water from a geyser. Now the light was coalescing. Focusing. Bending.

"It's making another arch," gasped Phil. She took a step back and craned her neck.

It was true. The light from the spinning medallion was curving like a rainbow now, reaching and bending overhead, growing quickly, silently, toward the opposite side.

Warren stared in awe as the tight column of multihued light touched down on the far bank of the stream. The new arch matched the old one perfectly in girth and span, and a gap of a foot or less separated the two structures.

"Many wonders have I witnessed," said Thaddeus softly, "but none to rival this."

"It's still changing," said Sean. "It's not done."

Warren watched. The unearthly rainbow was solidifying—transforming from a thing of light to a thing of stone—before their eyes. Warren saw with alarm that the stone was now growing around the flashing relic, encasing it. Sealing it. He reached for the medallion and smashed his hand against solid rock.

"Ow!" he cried.

He tried again. No use.

Within ten seconds the "arch of light" had become an arch of solid stone. An exact replica of the old arch, with one startling difference.

"You can still see the medallion!" cried Sean. "Look. You can see it spinning inside the rock."

It was true. Whether it was because the relic was so blindingly, dazzlingly brilliant, or because of some special property of the "stone" encasing it, the medallion could still be seen, pulsing like a beacon, deep inside the span.

"How do you get it back?" asked Sean.

Warren shook his head. "Probably like at the boulders. You get it back when it's ready to come back."

"Aye," said Thaddeus. "But attend, now. There's more to see."

Sean followed the big man's gaze. He was staring through the arches, to where the trail and chattering Angel Creek continued on the far side, and to the small clearing and forest beyond.

"It doesn't look any different," said the boy.

Warren and Phil stared, too. The country beyond did indeed look the same as ever. Same salal and huckleberry bushes. Same rocks. Same familiar campsites and fire rings under the trees a hundred feet ahead.

"Looks the same," Sean said, as if trying to convince himself.

"No," said Phil. She stepped forward with one hand outstretched. "It's all shimmery. See?"

She was right. The shimmer was subtle, but it was there. To Warren it felt as if he was staring through a sort of lens. A lens that made everything on the other side of the arch look just the tiniest bit bigger than normal. Warren looked up, then side to side, and saw that the "lens" filled the entire arch.

"It's sort of a ... window," said Phil. "But not like glass." "It's ... it's moving."

From arm's length, the "lens" looked like an impossibly delicate veil of falling water. A continuous, unbroken sheet of water filling the gap between the two arches and falling forever.

But it couldn't be water. There was no sound or spray. The ground was dry.

Standing in the center of the arch, in the middle of the trail that countless hikers had used, Phil touched the veil first. The tip of her finger penetrated the translucent barrier and vanished.

"Whoa!" she cried, and she jerked her hand back.

Warren stuck his arm through the veil, up to the elbow. The arm vanished, but the familiar landscape on the other side of the veil remained unchanged.

"The veil conceals another land," said Thaddeus, gazing at Warren's truncated arm in wonder.

"Shouldn't we … you know, put a stick through first?" stammered Sean. "Maybe send a dog? There's no telling what's really on the other side. What if you cross through and you can't get back? What if …"

Warren and Phil glanced at one another, clasped hands, and strode through the veil, vanishing utterly.

"Great," said Sean. "Thanks for listening."

"Let's have a look, lad," said Thaddeus, clasping Sean's shoulder. "You've come this far. Drive you mad, it will, if you don't have a look. Besides, we ain't got a dog."

They stepped through the barrier together and the universe changed.

Forty-five

Lights flashed, painfully bright; Warren cried out, and the veil enveloped him. It took two strides to pass through the barrier. The world went dark—though the flash lingered in his brain—and Warren felt a stabbing cold. A paralyzing, breathtaking cold. He clutched Phil's hand and kept moving.

The air warmed. Daylight returned, and there was an earthy, familiar smell. Warren blinked. "You okay?" he asked, his breath forming a frigid cloud in front of his face. Phil's hair was white with delicate ice crystals, and she was shivering.

"Yeah," she said. "You?" She released his hand.

"Fine. I think." They were standing inside a broad cave with rough, undulating walls.

Warm light poured through an opening just around the corner. Turning, they saw that the shimmering veil was still there, obscuring the back wall of the cave. *Or maybe the veil is the back wall,* Warren thought.

The veil warped and twisted suddenly and Thaddeus and Sean stumbled through, thoroughly ice-festooned themselves.

"Where are we?" gasped Sean, between shivers.

"Some kind of cave," said Warren.

"Not a cave," whispered Phil, who was touching a wall a few feet away. "It's living. It's … I think it's a tree. A hollow tree."

Warren touched another bit of wall curiously. Smooth wood. Tough, strong, ancient. It gave off a pungent, musty, earthy smell. "No tree's this big," he said, tracing the wall with his fingertips and craning his neck. The hollow was the size of his cabin.

"Not on Earth, anyway," said Thaddeus, stepping toward the light. The children followed, exited the tree—for that's indeed what it was—through a cleft in its colossal, sprawling trunk, and stepped into a meadow of wildflowers and deep, green grass.

There was much to see and absorb, and for a couple of minutes the four of them just stood in silence; turning, looking, staring.

To begin with, the tree was the largest living thing any of them had ever seen. By far.

The ancient, gnarled trunk rose over them like a castle wall. Thirty feet overhead, the trunk split into three stupendous limbs which arced gracefully, elegantly upward. These behemoths in turn split into thousands of lesser branches.

Warren gazed skyward. The tree was clearly ancient, but it was also healthy. Lush and full, vibrant and vigorous. Its canopy was vast—big enough to shade a football field. It reminded Warren of the broad-leafed maples he'd seen on the Seattle-side of the Cascades, though any normal maple would have resembled a Bonsai tree compared to this monster.

Warren wandered away from the tree, turning slowly as he walked, like a visitor entering the Great Hall at the Louvre. The tree, Warren saw, stood in the center of a sort of canyon, though it was unlike any canyon he'd ever seen.

Turning, Warren counted. The canyon had seven distinct faces: sheer, vertical walls of stone reaching hundreds of feet toward a deep blue sky. He counted again.

"A heptagon," he whispered, pointing at the walls as he rotated. "Like the medallion."

The canyon, or pit, as it seemed to Sean, was perhaps a half a mile across—roughly the size of a large city block—but seven-sided. The great tree, as far as they could tell, was the only tree in the entire canyon, and by far the most dominant feature. But it was not the only feature.

Twenty paces in front of the cleft in the trunk stood a monolith of stone, fifteen feet tall and similar in girth to the pillars of Stonehenge.

The monolith was decorated with crisp color images. Pictographs. Warren gave the drawings a quick glance before moving farther into the meadow, but Thaddeus seemed drawn to the standing stone. He stood before it, scrutinizing its dense, intricate images and periodically projecting quick bursts of bright, geometric holograms from his right eye.

"Where in blazes is Ina?" he muttered. "She ought to see this."

Forty-six

Two miles away, Ina was closing fast on Uhlgoth's last surviving Blank Frame. She waded through a narrow, brush-choked ravine, through walls of Devil's Club and stinging nettle; impediments that would have halted any ordinary hiker.

Dense fog cloaked the forest's emerald canopy, muting the light and making the hollows and recesses mysterious and forbidding. Visibility was fifty feet or less, but Ina wasn't relying on her eyes. Like Thaddeus and Achak, before he died, she could "see" and pinpoint other Fabrinels, even from miles away. Now her internal sensors told her that the last surviving Blank Frame lay behind a fallen tree at the bottom of the ravine, twenty paces ahead.

She plowed through a knot of spiny Devil's Club, and a burst of laser light pulsed from her left eye. The Blank

before her was huge. Probably one of Uhlgoth's elite Eltura Guard.

Like a cat, Ina leapt onto the massive deadfall and
scanned the moss-covered ground. There, amid the ferns,
an enormous Fabrinel arm lay outstretched. Pale. Lifeless.
Palm open. The rest of the creature was hidden beneath
the log.

Ina paused and opened the silver amulet hanging from
her neck. Molten-white cyber toxin lit up the forest. Carefully, she touched her knife to the substance and closed
the amulet.

This was it. The last Blank Frame. The last remnant of
Uhlgoth's invincible army. Once she'd destroyed it she
would run for Angel's Arch and plunge into the Center
Point.

Ina knew that Thaddeus and the children had found
the Center Point because she could no longer see Thaddeus on any of her maps or projections. His familiar signal had simply vanished from the world. She was eager to
rejoin her companions and—though she would never
have admitted it to Warren—eager to see the mysterious
Center Point for herself.

She leapt from the log, knife out, ready to stab the
flaccid arm as she hit the ground.

THWICK!

Like a snake, the arm suddenly recoiled.

The Blank wasn't dead! It was a trap. Somehow the
beast had concealed its true condition from Ina's sensors.
But now every molecule of her body was screaming the
alarm.

Too late.

Like an animal, the Eltura exploded from its hiding

place, smashed Ina against a tree, and impaled her with its long, cruel spear.

Ina jerked the spear loose and leapt for the enemy, but her legs shuddered beneath her and gave out.

The Fabrinel roared like a machine gun and Ina's world went dim. She saw yellow eyes. Flashing teeth. Pale, Plasticine flesh.

The Eltura swept up its glowing spear and swung around to deliver another blow. And Ina understood. To her horror, she realized the truth. This wasn't an ordinary Fabrinel or even an ordinary Eltura. It was something far more lethal.

"Thaddeus," she whispered, firing off one final communication as the creature lunged and the universe went black.

Ina's body withered into the ground and the Fabrinel's eyes glowed. It turned and sprinted for Angel's Arch.

Forty-seven

In the Center Point, Thaddeus was studying the monolith and Phil was staring into the distance.

Warren followed her gaze.

Embedded in one of the canyon's seven walls were stairs. Steps cut into the living rock: steep, precarious steps without railings or hand holds. The stairs climbed perhaps two hundred feet and ended in a dark opening. A "doorway" in the stone. Warm light poured from windows on either side of the doorway, but no people were visible.

"Someone lives here," said Phil.

"Or some *thing*," said Sean, eyeing the windows warily. "What is this place? Is it a Center Thingy?"

"Aye," said Thaddeus, lifting his gaze from the standing stone and turning to face the children.

"'Tis that. 'Tis everything the legends claim and more."

His eyes sparkled. "So much to see. So many possibilities. But we must very soon go back, I'm afraid."

"What?" said Warren. "Already?"

"Lad, you know we cannot stay. Think. The doorway is open." He gestured to the hollow in the great tree. "Soldiers are closing on Angel's Arch. We cannot risk them coming through and finding this."

"Todd Jr. said this place *was* the treasure," said Warren. "You said as much yourself."

"Oh lad, but it is," said Thaddeus. "Do you not savvy it? Do you not see the passageways and take their meaning?"

The children stared at him blankly.

"The tree," rumbled the big man impatiently. "Where we've come from just now—is of the Earth. Our Earth. Part of our universe."

The children stared at the tree.

"Now look at the canyon walls."

The children looked this way and that.

"Seven sheer walls. And what do they all have in common?"

Phil squinted at the nearest walls and answered first. "A cut?" she said. "An opening?"

"Aye," said Thaddeus. "Tracks radiating out from the train station, remember? Spokes in the wheel. Good lass."

Warren stared at the walls again. Phil was right. There was a crack in each of the seven faces, a narrow defile no wider than a foot path.

"Passageways?" said Sean. "But where do they lead?"

Thaddeus put his hand on his thigh and leaned toward the boy with an almost maniacal gleam in his eye. "Other worlds, lad. Have you not guessed it? Seven distinct, separate worlds." He looked at the children. "Have you forgotten all you've heard?

"When the Mendari visited four and a half centuries ago, they knew the Denelai were about to be wiped off the map by settlers moving west. The Mendari loved the Denelai. Wanted to protect them. Wanted to give them an escape route. A place to go, temporarily, where the cavalry couldn't follow. They gave them this." He stood erect and turned three hundred sixty degrees.

"Except," said Warren, "Uhlgoth attacked and the medallion was lost and no Denelai ever came here."

"That's what we thought," said the big man, eyes wide. He grabbed Warren by the arm and crossed with him to the Standing Stone. "But the pictures say otherwise. Someone *did* come. Long ago."

Warren spoke slowly. "But I found the medallion in our world."

"Aye," said Thaddeus. "I've thought of that. Maybe Annawan—the man you found—had been here. I heard naught of it, but maybe he had.

Warren studied the trail openings in the cliff walls. He loved trails—familiar ones and new ones—it didn't matter. There was a simple but palpable joy in discovering new territory around the next bend in a path. The idea that the mysterious, narrow trails surrounding them now led to different worlds—alien realms—was mind-blowing.

A gentle breeze rustled the great tree.

"But how is it better than gold?" asked Sean. "Or regular treasure?"

Thaddeus squinted at him. "Have ya gone dim, boy?

The seven pathways lead to seven worlds. *Worlds.* As in, planets. And not just any worlds, mind you. These are green, peaceful, human-friendly places special-chosen for the Denelai by the Mendari lords."

Sean turned slowly as Thaddeus's words sank in. "Oh," he said.

"Seven worlds," said Phil. "One for each gem on the medallion."

"Aye."

"The Denelai would've missed Onatah," said Warren.

"Aye," said Thaddeus. "This weren't intended as a replacement for Earth, but as a refuge. A hideaway—until The People could return home.

"Are they in our galaxy then?" asked Phil. "The worlds?"

"P'raps not. P'raps not even in our universe." Thaddeus's speech quickened, as if he'd just heard a summons no one else could hear. "Center Point can lead anywhere. There's no tellin' and there's no time to find out. We must be off."

Warren didn't want to leave. "But can't we just look at one of the paths? Real quick? Just go a few paces in?"

"Forget it, lad," said Thaddeus. "We've lingered too long as it stands. I fear what we may find on the other side of the veil. Follow me."

The big man gave a quick, final glance around the strange, silent meadow and strode toward the cleft in the great tree.

The children followed. Phil came last and a sudden flicker of movement high on the canyon wall caught her eye. She froze.

It was the wall with the stairs and lofty chamber. A shape inside the chamber flitted past a window. Someone had been watching them. But the windows were empty now and she turned and sprinted for the tree. The others had already vanished inside the trunk.

Forty-eight

Todd Jr. and Manuel were well clear of the boulders, fiddling with gear and looking in the opposite direction. Finley was still in the bay.

Thaddeus was the first to emerge from the Center Point—the first to cross back through the shimmering veil and stumble from Angel's Arch.

To Thaddeus and the children it was a passage from darkness to light. From the black interior of the hollow tree to the muted daylight of the Staircase Trail.

To an observer standing on the terrestrial side of Angel's Arch, it would have seemed a thing of magic or hallucination: a bearded giant popping out of thin air, followed in rapid succession by three grimy, disheveled children.

As soon as the mountain man set foot on familiar ground, he knew something had gone horribly wrong.

"I-NA!" he cried, staggering and choking on her name. "I-NA!" He howled, voice broken and pitiful. "Oh no! No! No! It cannot be!"

"What is it?" cried Warren, scanning the clearing around the arch. The fog hung heavy and low, as before, and there was no one in sight. "What happened?"

"I-NA!" sobbed the big man, clutching his head like a madman and staggering through the grass.

Phil caught him and put her arm around his waist. "What about Ina?" she said firmly. "What's happened?"

"She's dead," sobbed Thaddeus.

"Dead?"

"What?" cried Warren. "How? And how do you know?"

Thaddeus steadied himself. "We have to leave," he gasped.

"But ..."

"Now. There is great danger afoot." The big man glanced quickly about, then turned to Warren. "Lad. Retrieve the medallion. Hurry!"

Warren nodded and looked to The Pedestal. The twinkling medallion was still encased in stone, inside the identical twin span of Angel's Arch, but it was becoming more visible by the moment.

The duplicate arch had seemed as solid as the original before they crossed to the Center Point, but now the new arch was fading. Dissolving. And Warren noticed something else: the shimmering veil was getting thinner, more transparent, harder to see. He stepped to the pedestal and reached tentatively for the twirling relic.

"FREEZE!" boomed a voice. A confident, powerful,

female voice. "Everybody freeze! FBI!"

Warren withdrew his hand from the pedestal and turned slowly toward the forest.

A tall, fit young woman stepped from the trees and leveled her gun on Thaddeus. The woman wore an FBI vest and ball cap. Her skin glistened with sweat.

Warren saw her eyes sweep the meadow as she struggled to make sense of the bizarre scene: the bearded giant in 1820s garb. The ragamuffin kids. The rapidly fading arch.

"FBI!" she declared again, slightly less confidently. "Hands in the air! Now!"

Warren and the other children started to comply, when a shape exploded from the brush twenty yards behind the pedestal.

The shape was moving so fast Warren thought at first it was a cougar or bear in full charge. Then it cleared the undergrowth and Warren gasped. It was a Fabrinel. An enormous, yellow-eyed Blank Frame.

Straight for the arch the creature leapt, shrieking and clicking as it came; Ina's turquoise and silver amulet swinging from its neck.

Thaddeus howled with rage and lunged to intercept. His enormous hunting knife flashed like a mirror.

"Freeze!" shrieked the FBI agent. And then she fired on Thaddeus, and the roar of her gun ricocheted around the narrow valley: *BOOM! BOOM! BOOM! BOOM!*

Warren spun, and the next few seconds unfolded like a nightmare.

Bullets smashed into Thaddeus and had not the slightest effect. Straight for the Fabrinel the mountain man charged, a murderous juggernaut bent on revenge.

The Blank Frame darted left, side-stepped Thaddeus, and smashed like a bull into the pedestal. It groped for the medallion.

CLICK! The medallion broke free from its invisible mount. The beast swung hard around—avoiding Thaddeus's knife by a centimeter—and lunged toward the quickly disappearing veil.

The beast would've leapt alone into the Center Point. But Phil stood in its path.

With a roar, the creature flattened the girl, knocking her back through the shimmering curtain.

"Phil!" Warren cried. But beast and girl were gone.

Warren caught a glimpse of the FBI agent sprinting toward him and Sean. Other FBI and military people were pouring from the forest now, and Thaddeus was a great blur leaping for the veil.

Warren felt his mother calling from the edge of the clearing. Even over the cacophony and confusion, her voice cut through, telling him to be careful, telling him goodbye.

There was no time for discussion. No time to weigh the options or consider the circumstances. Warren looked at Sean, and in a millisecond they agreed; and jumped. And for a terrible, heart-seizing moment, Warren wondered if they would even make it through.

The Fabrinel had taken the medallion, and the duplicate arch was fading fast. Nothing but a mirage of it remained. The translucent veil had gone perilously thin. In a moment it would not exist at all.

Thaddeus plowed through and the boys leapt after—

pushing this time—fighting their way through the vanishing door. FBI agent Hanna Walker came last.

The duplicate arch vanished. The veil disappeared. And the fog in the little meadow began to lift.

Also by the Author

The Gaia Wars

Exodus 2018 (Coming Soon)

About the Author

Kenneth G. Bennett is also the author of *The Gaia Wars*, and the forthcoming *Exodus 2018*, a paranormal thriller set in the Puget Sound region of Washington State.

Ken lives on an island in the Pacific Northwest, with his wife and son.

Visit Ken at kennethgbennett.com. And learn more about *The Gaia Wars* at thegaiawars.com